Her life would never be the same again....

Emma carefully removed the lace, and there it was. An odd arc of dull gold. She touched it, and received a small shock. Emma shrank back, as if the thing were dangerous. Absurd. She picked up the heavy gold piece and held it in her palm.

It was obviously something of value, for her mother had kept it all these years. She had no idea what it was, but she was certain of one thing. Her search was over. This strange curve of gold tubing was what she was looking for. "Look for the owl," her mother had told her—and there it was. At least, part of one.

For one end of the gold arc flattened into a distinct shape: that of a single spread wing and one half of an eerie, wise-looking owl's head and body. From the strange split face sparkled a lone emerald eye. Emma stared at it, transfixed. An unexpected sense of foreboding overcame her. For some reason the odd warning of the old gypsy woman popped into her head: "The world as you know it is about to be turned upside down."

Emma had found the owl, and she knew—without knowing why—that her life would never be the same again.

Emerald's Desire

PAULA MUNIER LEE

All characters appearing in this work are fictitious. Any resemblance to real persons, living or dead, is purely coincidental.

Produced by Alloy Entertainment
1325 Avenue of the Americas
New York, NY 10019
www.alloyentertainment.com

Reprint edition 2016

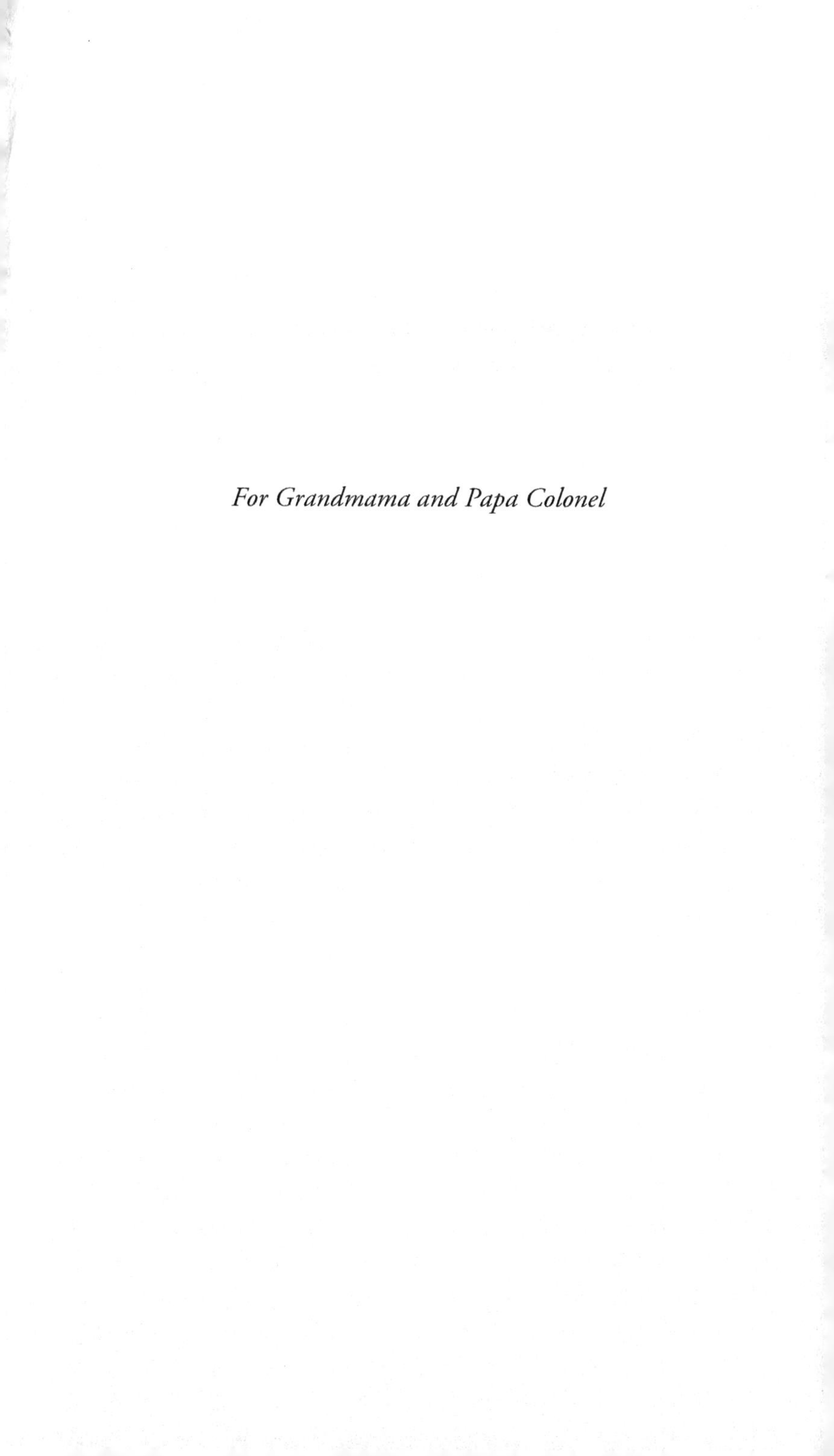

For Grandmama and Papa Colonel

How sweetly lies old Ireland
Emerald green beyond the foam,
Awakening sweet memories,
Calling the heart back home.

—*An Irish blessing*

Chapter One

She didn't even recognize him at first. Perched dangerously on the edge of a police barricade, Emma swung her Nikon camera around just in time to snap a shot of the St. Columba High School band as they marched down State Street, drums rolling and trumpets blaring.

A tall young man stepped in front of her, blocking the spectacular view of the St. Patrick's Day parade Emma was risking life and limb for. She didn't mean to be rude, but she'd gotten up at four A.M. to get there early enough to secure a good picture-taking spot. She waved her free arm at him. "Move! Please!"

"Emma?" The young man planted himself in front of her lens and refused to move. "Emma Lambourne?" He raised his voice against the rising clamor of the approaching band.

Emma ignored him. She leaned to the right, twisting her torso in a last-ditch effort to get a second shot of the marching band. Her right eye fixed to the viewfinder, she realized she need only move another couple of inches to clear the frame. She arched her back, tilting toward the band. Just as she clicked the shutter button she lost her footing. She teetered on the slim edge of the barricade and fell forward—right into the arms of the persistent young man.

He caught her easily, and set her down on the crowded street beside him. "Emma," he said, smiling, "it *is* you."

Emma frowned at him, then checked her camera, which dangled from her shoulder by a thick leather strap. "It seems to be okay," she said, more to herself than to him.

"What about you?"

She looked up at him, considering him carefully for the first time. He was tall and well built, around her age, maybe older. Nineteen or twenty, she guessed. His sandy hair fell over his forehead, framing a open face with even features, brightened by deep blue eyes that smiled at her as if he knew her well. There was something familiar about him, but she couldn't pinpoint exactly what.

"Emma, are you all right?"

"I'm fine, really." She looked at him again, trying to place him. "Do I know you?"

"You don't remember me."

"You seem familiar somehow, but—"

"That's okay. It's been a while." He paused. "Sam Tyler, from Kenilworth High. I graduated last year." He offered her his hand, and she shook it absently as she stared at him.

"Sammy?" Emma couldn't believe it. This was not the Sammy she knew from the school paper, the skinny, awkward techno-weenie who was always taking her perfectly composed photos and altering them to suit his own purposes on that fancy computer of his. Oh, he was talented enough, but what a nerd! She looked at the guy who stood smiling at her now. This was no nerd. "Sure, now I remember. It's been so long... what have you been up to?"

"I'm studying computer art at the University of Chicago."

"That's great." Emma smiled at him, not knowing what to say next.

Sam grinned back at her. "So I guess you're still hard at work on the photography. You were always so good. I didn't mean to interrupt—"

"That's okay," Emma said, watching the backs of the St. Columba High School band members as they continued their noisy march down State Street. "No problem; another band will be along any minute."

"I know better. Listen, how about I make it up to you?"

Emma cast him a doubtful look. "How?"

Sam pointed to the barricade. "That's not the safest place, you know. I've got a better idea. Hold on to your camera." With that he scooped her up and set her down on his shoulders.

"What are you doing?" Emma said with a laugh. This bold new Sam certainly had changed a lot in just a year.

"How's the view up there?"

"Fine." The truth was, the view was great. Emma raised her camera to her eye and snapped away at the Cork County Gaelic Dancers as they jigged and whirled their way past them. She caught one lively redhead in mid-pirouette, her petticoats flying, green and white lace flashing. Perfect.

Emma spent the rest of the parade on Sam's shoulders, shooting roll after roll of film. More than an hour later, the festivities began to wind down. She knew he must be getting tired, but she was having such a good time that she didn't want to stop. She had never felt so comfortable with such a cute guy before. Maybe that was because this cute guy was really Sammy the techno-weenie in disguise.

She wished Sally were there. Sally was her favorite cousin in a large family of cousins; they'd been best friends all their lives. The blue-eyed blonde attracted guys without even trying—she was a master of the fine art of flirting. Emma never had been much good at flirting. Sally always said she was too direct. She was right, of course, but still it was the only way Emma knew. She decided to plunge right in.

"Look," she said as Sam helped her back down to the ground, "you've been such a help. Let me treat you to lunch." She smiled at him like Sally always smiled at her guys. "It'll be my way of saying thank you."

"That's not necessary. It was my pleasure, really."

"I insist," Emma said, abandoning Sally's smile and replacing it with a more genuine one of her own. "I know a little café over on Flaherty where we can get a great corned beef sandwich."

Sam smiled back. "Sounds good." He took her hand and they began to walk.

The final police escort rumbled past them, a noisy cavalcade of motorcycles. A troupe of peddlers followed in their wake, selling all manner of St. Patrick's Day souvenirs, from shamrock balloons to Emerald Isle T-shirts. Emma and Sam traveled along with them, Emma snapping close-ups of the peddlers and their Irish wares while Sam pointed out new subjects.

They cut over to Michigan Avenue, then headed north to Flaherty. At Colleen's, the little café, the staff had taken advantage of the unseasonably warm, sunny weather and moved some tables outside on the summer patio that flanked the sidewalk. A trio of fiddlers serenaded the patrons with Gaelic folk songs, while an old gypsy read tarot cards in the corner.

Sam pulled out a chair for Emma at a small table near the old gypsy woman. "This is a great place."

Emma smiled. "I've always loved it." She opened her arms to embrace the air. "Not just this restaurant, but the whole street. These old Irish neighborhoods fascinate me."

Sam looked at her with wry eyes. "A little more colorful than our own Kenilworth, isn't it?"

Emma frowned. "Don't get me wrong. I love Kenilworth. It's home. But compared to all this, it's so ... so ... "

"Sterile?"

"Yes, sterile."

"I know what you mean." Sam leaned across the table. "I couldn't wait to get out of the suburbs. That's why I chose the University of Chicago, so I could be downtown, where the action is."

Emma considered this. "I bet your parents didn't like that much."

"Of course not. They wanted me to go to Northwestern in Evanston."

"It's the Kenilworth thing to do." Kenilworth, where Emma lived with her mother in a picture-perfect house on a picture-perfect street, was a very wealthy suburb far north of the city of Chicago proper. It was her hometown, but she longed to escape, as Sam had.

"Are you planning to do the Kenilworth thing?"

Emma sighed. "I don't know. I'd like to go to California to study photography at Brooks. But I haven't made any real plans yet. ... "

"You should. You'll be graduating in a couple of months. There's a big, beautiful world out there—far away from Kenilworth High."

Emma knew Sam was right. She would have to make a decision about college soon, but she hesitated to bring the subject up with her mother. Emma's father had died when she was little; her mother was an only child whose parents had passed away years before. Emma was all her mother had left. She dreaded the thought of going off to school and leaving her mother all alone.

The waiter brought their corned beef sandwiches, and Emma and Sam fell into an easy silence as they ate their late lunch together.

After they finished, Sam pointed to the gypsy woman. "Come on, let's have her tell your fortune. She'll prove to you that there really is life after high school."

Emma shook her head. "I don't believe in that stuff."

"You always were such a skeptic." Then Sam tempted her with the one thing she couldn't resist. "Let her read your fortune and she may sit still for a couple of close-ups."

Emma smiled. She couldn't believe he remembered so much about her. He must have been paying a lot more attention to her than she had to him, she thought, feeling flattered and a little guilty. "Your treat?"

"My treat."

"You've got a deal."

Emma paid the check and then allowed Sam to escort her to the gypsy's table. The old woman certainly looked the part in her flowing skirts and gold turban. She wore a multitude of gold necklaces and bracelets, which jingled and jangled every time she shuffled her tarot cards. Her small black eyes brightened as she waved Emma into the seat across from her.

"My name is Madame Rose," she announced, and then stared openly at Emma.

Emma grew restless under the old woman's intense gaze. "What do I do?"

"Concentrate on the light within you." The gypsy laid the tarot cards facedown across the red felt tablecloth, spreading them out like a fan in a long arc. Celtic crosses against a bright mosaic pattern decorated the backs of the cards.

Emma found the old woman's serious manner amusing. Out of the corner of her eye she caught Sam looking at her, and she winked at him.

"It is important to concentrate," scolded the gypsy.

"I know," said Emma, "on the light within."

"A young woman of your background should take this more seriously," Madame Rose told her sternly.

Emma grinned. "And what background would that be?"

"You are descended from the Irish kings and queens of Tara."

"Right." Emma laughed, knowing that her family was English, not Irish. All of the Lambournes were blond, blue-eyed Britons like Sally; she was the only exception, thanks to some errant gene on her mother's side. Emma's paternal grandmother, Beatrice, proudly traced her lineage back to Queen Elizabeth I, and would deny to her death any remote ties to the Irish—or any non-Anglo-Saxons, for that matter. Beatrice would consider this old woman's words insulting to the family name—not that she'd approve of Emma having her tarot read by a gypsy in the first place. She wouldn't approve of anything that happened in that neighborhood.

"You can't deny it," said Madame Rose defensively, "not with those green eyes and that red hair."

Emma smiled at the old woman. She hadn't meant to offend her. "I'm sorry. Let's go on with the reading."

"Close your eyes, my dear."

Emma did as she was told.

"Now, visualize a soft white light. Let the light envelop you. Become one with the light."

To spare the old woman's feelings, Emma pretended to concentrate. She sat in silence and waited. Even with her eyes closed she could feel the old woman's dark gaze upon her.

"Good," said Madame Rose. "You may open your eyes now, but try to hold on to the light."

Emma opened her eyes. She watched the gypsy woman as she slowly pulled a card from the middle of the half moon of tarot cards spread before her.

"The Tower," said Madame Rose in a hushed voice.

"What does it mean?" Emma asked with mock solemnity, playing along.

"The Tower symbolizes destruction." She sighed. "Never a good card to pull. But just how terrible the destruction will be we won't know until we pull the other cards." Madame Rose quickly drew two more cards, one from each end of the tarot fan. She turned the one on the right over, and shuddered. "The Hanged Man." She looked up at Emma, deep lines of concern creasing her forehead.

"More bad news?" asked Emma lightly.

"The world as you know it is about to be turned upside down."

"Great." Emma grinned at Sam. "Guess you were wrong, Sam. There is no life after high school. At least not for me." Emma got up to go. "Thank you, Madame Rose."

"Wait," said Madame Rose, "the third card." She placed the last card faceup. "Strength," she said, sighing in relief. "The Strength card means you will survive, if you are strong."

"Great. Thanks again." Emma grabbed her camera and snapped a couple of shots of the old woman and the tarot cards.

"You must be strong to survive," repeated Madame Rose.

"No problem." Emma turned to go. She'd had enough of this mumbo jumbo; she wanted some time alone with Sam before she had to go home, which was pretty soon.

"Ten dollars, please."

Emma laughed. "Reward Madame Rose, Sam. She says I'll survive life after high school, after all."

Sam slipped the old woman a twenty. "Keep the change," he told her.

"Good-bye, Madame Rose." Emma bowed slightly to the old woman, then swung her camera to her shoulder. She was ready to go. Sam once again took her hand in his and they proceeded down the street.

Emma had already forgotten the old woman when she heard Madame Rose calling after her, "Be strong, my child!"

CHAPTER TWO

"Where to now?" Sam asked as they continued down Flaherty Street.

"The train station," answered Emma reluctantly. "I've got to get home."

"Okay."

"You don't have to come with me, you know," Emma said, hoping he would. "I know where the train station is."

"It's on my way."

Emma wasn't sure she believed that, but she didn't care. Running into Sam had been the highlight of the day—a day she almost hated to end. If he wanted to hang around a little longer, that was fine with her.

They walked together in silence through the streets of Chicago. It was nearing dusk now, and growing chilly. They crossed over the bridge that led to the station, shivering as a blast of cold air from Lake Michigan hit them hard. They ran for the warm respite of the station. Once inside, Sam walked Emma to the tracks, where the northbound train was about to depart for the suburbs.

"Thanks for all your help."

"No problem. It was great seeing you again."

Emma felt suddenly ill at ease. She didn't want to leave, but she had to go home. She didn't know what to say. So she didn't say anything.

"You'd better get on the train."

"Yeah." Disappointed, Emma turned to go. She'd hoped Sam would say something about getting together again, but she knew that was unrealistic. After all, running into him that day had been strictly an accident. He seemed glad enough to see her, sure, but he was a college man now. He had thousands of college women to choose from at the university. She was just a kid he knew from high school.

Emma stepped up into the commuter train. "Goodbye, Sam. Thanks again."

"Bye." Sam smiled at her as the doors began to close between them. "Can I call you sometime?"

Emma grinned. "Sure. Anytime." She made her way to a seat in the nonsmoking car to her left. She sat by the window, hoping for a glimpse of Sam as he left the station.

To her surprise he was still standing there, smiling at her. She slipped her camera out of its case and removed the lens cap. Raising the lens to the glass, she focused on Sam, snapping a series of shots as the train slowly pulled out of the station.

It was a long ride home through the outlying neighborhoods of the city, then up through the many suburbs that bordered the shore of Lake Michigan: Evanston, Winnetka, and finally home to Kenilworth.

Within twenty minutes the gentle swaying of the train lulled Emma into a troubled sleep. She dreamed of marching bands and shamrocks and gypsies, Irish dancers and tarot cards and corned beef sandwiches. Then this kaleidoscope of images whirled into a new reality, and Emma found herself at the top of an ancient tower high on a hill, staring down into a sea of darkness. Suddenly lightning filled the sky, striking the tower with an electric jolt. Emma felt the old masonry crumble beneath her. She lost her footing and tumbled headfirst into the swirling blackness beneath her.

"Kenilworth station, Kenilworth station!"

The booming voice of the conductor over the train's public address system broke into Emma's dream, awakening her.

Home, she thought with relief. She gathered up her gear and left the train. It was dark now, nearly suppertime. Emma hurried through the station to the parking lot, where her blue Jeep Cherokee awaited. Her mother had presented her with the rugged vehicle on her sixteenth birthday. Emma loved it because she could pack a lot of camera equipment in it and drive it anywhere, fast.

She zipped away from the station and drove the two miles home through the wide, tree-lined streets of Kenilworth. A small, exclusive enclave of the rich and very rich, Kenilworth prided itself on tasteful extravagance. The residents of Kenilworth had the best of everything, but they didn't flaunt it. No flashy nouveau riche elements here, just lots of old money spent in the old way—quietly.

The houses were grand but sedate; their owners were snobbish but subtly so.

Emma pulled into the driveway of the house she'd lived in all her life. It was a tasteful home of beige brick set on a large expanse of lawn and framed by tall silver birches. Her father had built it for her mother before Emma was born; after he died of cancer when Emma was two, she and her mother had stayed on there. Her mother had always refused to sell the house, saying that it was all she had left of him. She had never married again—had never even dated. Emma had no memory of her father, but she often wished she could remember the man who had inspired such selfless love and devotion in her mother.

Emma grabbed her camera gear and headed for the house. She couldn't wait to tell her mother about her day.

"Mama!" Emma walked through the long entry, which was lined with Emma's photographs, artfully framed by Emma's mother. Emma's mother had turned the beige walls of her graceful home into a gallery for her daughter. She proudly displayed every photo suitable for framing that Emma had ever taken—beginning with the shots she had taken with her first roll of film on her tenth birthday, when her mother had presented her with a little Kodak.

The gallery reflected the two loves of Emma's life: her mother and the old Irish neighborhoods of Chicago.

There was her mother playing Chopin on the baby grand piano Emma's father had given her as a wedding present; her mother tending her beloved La Reine

Victoria roses; her mother reading her favorite book, Jane Austen's *Pride and Prejudice.* She was a solitary, serene woman—and Emma had tried to capture her stillness in these soft, ethereal portraits.

The photographs of life in Chicago's old Irish neighborhoods were altogether different. These were color and black-and-white shots of all things Gaelic: bagpipers and jig dancers and clergy in Celtic crosses; Virgin Mary statues and St. Patrick holy medals and good-luck shamrocks; parades and church suppers and block parties. These cheerful, lively photos revealed an energy that seemed out of place in that house, in that neighborhood.

Every time Emma's grandmother came to call—which wasn't often—she would remark to Emma's mother, "Grace, I don't know why you encourage this little hobby of Emma's by hanging these unfortunate portraits where the world can see them." Her grandmother did not believe any photography qualified as art—especially Emma's.

Her mother always ignored such remarks, if indeed she heard them at all. She supported her daughter in all things, even when the formidable Grandmother Beatrice disapproved.

Emma continued through the house, stopping in the kitchen to pour a glass of orange juice. There she found a note on the refrigerator: *Emma darling—Bridge night. Back by ten. Love, Mom.* Once a month Grandmother Beatrice invited the ladies in the Lambourne family over for bridge—sort of a command performance.

Her mother hated bridge, but she went anyway. For her daughter's sake, Emma suspected, more than her own. Since she had no family, her mother thought it was important for Emma to be close to her father's family. "There's nothing more important than family," Emma's mother always told her. "Family is everything."

Emma carried the glass along with her camera gear up the stairs to her bedroom, a tasteful young lady's retreat decorated by her mother but made Emma's own by a clutter of Irish souvenirs, Celtic art, and photographic paraphernalia. She'd been collecting all things Irish since her first St. Patrick's Day parade, when she was just a little girl. She disappeared into the walk-in closet, which her mother had helped her to turn into a darkroom when she was thirteen. The darkroom had become her sanctuary, where she honed her technical skills and developed her eye as an artist.

Like most photographers, Emma sent her color rolls to a professional photo lab for processing, but saved the developing of the black-and-white shots for herself. Though she enjoyed her color prints, she preferred working in black and white. The play of light and shadow, the simplicity of hues, the elemental drama of this medium intrigued Emma.

Luckily, she thought as she set up her chemicals to develop her day's work, *that last roll was black and white.* This meant she could develop the shots of Sam that same night. She couldn't wait to see them; she believed black-and-white photos revealed a person's character in a way color never could. She wanted to get a good look at the real Sam.

Despite her excitement, Emma forced herself to develop the rest of the photos first. She worked deliberately, bringing to life in the darkroom the striking likenesses of the drum majorette of the St. Columba High School band, the Cork County Gaelic Dancers, Madame Rose and her strange tarot cards. Emma shivered; for some reason the thought of the old woman unsettled her. Amazed at her reaction, she shook off the feeling and went back to work.

Engrossed in her photography, Emma lost all track of time. Hours had passed by the time she hung up the last shots on the last roll to dry. She stood back to admire her handiwork.

Sam's smiling face shone out at her in the darkness. Even under the surreal darkroom lighting, the series of black-and-white shots revealed an earnest young man of good character. Good-looking, but not gorgeous. Confident, but not arrogant.

Sam had a face Emma could trust. Her pictures proved it.

Emma smiled in satisfaction, then hurried to tidy up her work space. Her mother would be home soon, and she wanted to show her these photos of Sam. If she didn't dawdle, she'd have time to take a quick shower before her mother arrived.

The phone was ringing when Emma stepped out of the shower. She wrapped a thick towel around her torso, then ran to answer it. It was Sally, checking in for their nightly call, in which they told each other everything that had happened that day. Since the ever-popular Sally's days were much fuller than Emma's, Sally typically dominated these conversations. She began as she usually did, with a detailed retelling of her St. Patrick's Day activities.

"I played tennis with Mark Jeffers this morning, beat him in three straight sets ... Jason Harrington took me to the parade and out to lunch at the club afterward ... and then Bryan Rollins picked me up at seven. We went to that new Christian Slater movie—now there's a hunk for you. Bryan's okay, but he's no Christian Slater." Sally sighed. "I don't think there's anybody that cute in Illinois. You probably have to go to Hollywood to meet guys like that." Sally sighed again. "So how was your day? Get any good shots?"

"As a matter of fact I did."

"Good for you."

"You won't believe who I ran into down there."

"Christian Slater."

Emma laughed. "Not exactly. But close."

"Who?"

"Sam Tyler. You remember, he graduated last year."

"Of course. He's at the University of Chicago now, majoring in computer graphics."

Emma laughed again. When it came to guys, Sally was a walking encyclopedia. "What else can you tell me about him?"

"You're interested in Sam Tyler?" Sally sounded stunned.

"Well," said Emma defensively, "he's changed a lot since high school."

"I'll say. I saw him with Tiffany Thompson at a party a couple of months ago. Talk about transformations. ... "

Sally rambled on, but Emma wasn't listening. Tiffany Thompson was a beautiful girl nearly as popular as Sally. "Is she his girlfriend?"

"Who?"

"Tiffany Thompson. Is she Sam's girlfriend?"

"Oh, no. Tiffany's with Jack Donner now—you know, the heir to the Donner fortune. Very dull, but very rich."

"What about Sam?"

"What about him?"

"Who's he with?"

"Nobody, as far as I know." Sally giggled. "I can't believe this. You really are interested in this guy, aren't you?"

"Well—"

"You are human after all. Thank God. Now tell me everything that happened to you two today, from the beginning. And don't leave anything out."

Emma spent the next half hour satisfying Sally's insatiable curiosity. When she finally hung up, she slipped into her pajamas and brushed her long, heavy red hair, still wet from the shower. She was on her way downstairs for a snack when she heard the doorbell ring. Glancing at the clock, she realized it was after eleven. Who would drop by so late? And where was her mother? She should have been home an hour before.

Emma scurried down the stairs in her bare feet. She started to open the door, then thought better of it. Instead, she peeked through the peephole, as her mother had instructed her.

It was a police officer. Panic seized Emma's heart, and she threw open the door.

"Are you Miss Lambourne?"

"Yes," Emma answered uncertainly, afraid to ask why he was there.

"You'd better come with me," the police officer told her. "There's been an accident."

Emma hated hospitals. She hated the artificial white gleam of the walls and the floors and the ceilings. She hated the antiseptic smell that masked the fearful odors of sickness and death. Most of all, she hated the way she felt whenever she walked into one: scared.

She was scared now. On the way over in the police car, the officer had explained to her that her mother had been hurt badly in a car accident.

"She was blindsided by an eighteen-wheeler," he said. "The man who was driving the truck died instantly."

"What happened?" Emma pictured her poor mother trapped in a crush of metal.

"He blew a tire and lost control of the vehicle," said the officer. "Just one of those things."

Just one of those things. Emma said a silent prayer for her mother.

Once at the hospital, the police officer left her with the head nurse in intensive care, who smiled at her sadly.

"Your mother has suffered severe internal injuries," the nurse told her. "We have her in intensive care, which means you can see her for only five minutes every hour. She's very weak. Do you understand?"

Emma nodded. The nurse took her arm gently and led her down a long hall to a small room filled with medical equipment Emma had never seen before. Her mother lay on a narrow bed, hooked up to the imposing machines. Her eyes were closed.

"Is she—" Emma's voice broke. Her mother looked pale, too pale. Her short blond hair fell listlessly over her forehead. "Is she—" Fear rooted Emma to the shiny white floor.

"She's alive," the nurse said quietly. "But we can't make any promises. We've done all we can. She's in God's hands now." She patted Emma on the shoulder. "Go on, dear."

The nurse left and Emma was alone with her mother. She gathered her courage and moved toward the bed. Standing there at her mother's side, she looked down at the one person in the world she loved the most, the one person in the world she couldn't live without.

"Oh, Mama." Emma took her mother's cool, pale hand and held it in her own. "Don't die, Mama. Don't leave me."

Her mother's eyelids fluttered.

Emma's heart leapt. "Mama?" She leaned forward. "Can you hear me?"

Her mother opened her eyes and winced. "Emma."

Emma squeezed her hand. "Don't talk, Mama. Just hold on."

A shudder shook her mother's thin frame. "Emma, listen to me." Her gray eyes searched Emma's face. "There's something I must tell you."

"Rest, Mama. Whatever you want to say can wait."

"No." Her mother's beautiful voice was reduced to a hoarse whisper.

"Shh, Mama, shh." Emma gently brushed the limp curls from her mother's pallid forehead.

"Listen." Desperation crept into her mother's voice.

"I'm listening, Mama," Emma said, chastened.

"There's something I should have told you a long time ago." Her mother struggled to sit up. "You need to know now." Exhausted, she fell back against her pillow.

"Don't move, Mama." Emma slipped her arms around her mother's shoulders and supported her.

"You need to know," her mother whispered.

"Shh. Save your strength."

Her mother looked at her, her cheeks wet with tears. "There's no time. ... " She shuddered and shut her eyes.

"Mama—" Emma was crying now, too. "Mama—"

Her mother opened her eyes once more. "I can't leave you all alone," she told Emma. "Look for the owl." Her eyes closed again. She sighed and was suddenly very still.

As she held her mother, willing her to live, Emma felt her slipping away. She died then, quietly, and Emma cradled her in her arms and wept.

Chapter Three

The next few days passed in a terrible blur. Against everybody's advice—the police's, Sally's, and the school counselor's—Emma insisted on staying at the house, alone.

Several people offered to take her in, or to stay there in the house with her, but she refused. She had just lost her mother, and no one, friend or family, could comfort her. She didn't want consolation, she didn't want to talk about her feelings, she just wanted to be alone.

The only person who seemed to understand was Sally, who guarded Emma's privacy with the tenacity of a blond pit bull. Sally was used to getting her own way; as she was Grandmother Beatrice's favorite, no one dared defy her. She succeeded in keeping everyone away from Emma, saying, "I don't care whether you approve or not; it's what Emma wants, and that's good enough for me."

Sally also ran interference between Emma and Grandmother Beatrice, who at Emma's request was making all the funeral arrangements. Sally had suggested this, and Emma was grateful to her for it. She didn't know anything about funerals. Her grandmother was very concerned with appearances; you could always count on her to do the proper thing. Grandmother Beatrice also spared Emma the terrible task of communicating the news to friends and family, and accepted their condolences on her behalf.

Emma simply wasn't up to dealing with the huge cast of great-aunts and great-uncles and second cousins that peopled family tragedies. She didn't want to talk to anybody. She just wanted to go to sleep, finish this horrible dream, and wake up again to her mother's smiling face.

That's how the whole situation struck Emma—as if it were some slow-motion dream. Each scene was more horrific than the next, culminating in the funeral, a Gothic nightmare held in St. Paul's Episcopalian Church in Kenilworth, all of the many Lambournes and most of the local residents in attendance.

Emma sat in the front row with Grandmother Beatrice and Sally. She wore an expensive high-necked black wool dress and too-tight high-heeled black leather pumps her grandmother had bought her especially for this awful occasion. She was allergic to wool, and so the dress made her itch. Sitting there in the church, she could feel the welts forming across her back and chest and up her arms and neck. She didn't mind; she was so full of emotional pain that she almost welcomed the physical pain—it was so much easier to bear.

She knew her grandmother was watching her every move, keeping one stern eye on the minister and one on her. All her life her grandmother had watched her that way—she was as intolerant of Emma's faults as she was forgiving of Sally's. Ever since they were little girls, Sally had charmed their grandmother with her innate poise and personality. Emma, on the other hand, had always been shy and awkward and incapable of pleasing Grandmother Beatrice. Even after she had grown up, the old woman's scrutiny usually made Emma nervous, but that day she barely noticed. She was held fast by her grief, conscious of nothing but the gaping hole in her heart.

Psalms and hymns and mourners swirled around her, and the smell of incense hung in the air. The chapel was dark and cold; outside a hard March rain battered the stained-glass windows.

The minister droned on about the Valley of Death. Emma felt the high walls of the church folding in on her. People crowded her, pews squeezed her, the very air enveloped her.

She couldn't breathe. She gasped for air, but still she couldn't breathe. She could feel Grandmother Beatrice's stare on her, but she didn't care. She had to get out of there.

"Emma, what's wrong?" Sally whispered.

Emma bolted from her seat and stumbled down the center aisle. Blindly she ran out of the building into the bracing rain. There she stopped and stood on the stone steps of the tall church, gulping air and swallowing water. Within seconds she was drenched to the skin; the scratchy black wool dress clung to her every pore. She slipped off the high heels and sat down on the top step. She closed her eyes and lifted her wet head to the wind. Rain washed over her face, mingling with the tears she'd kept bottled up inside all morning.

"Emma?"

She felt a warm hand on her cold shoulder. She sighed. Why couldn't they just leave her alone?

"Emma," the voice repeated.

They weren't going to leave her alone after all. With reluctance Emma opened her eyes.

There stood Sam, all dressed up in Kenilworth style—dark blue suit, white shirt, red tie. He was as wet as she was; his fine sandy hair was plastered to his forehead. He looked at her with concern. "Are you all right?"

"You're getting all wet," Emma said.

Sam smiled kindly at her. "Look who's talking."

"Your suit is ruined."

"I never liked it much anyway. Look, you're going to catch pneumonia out here." Sam took her gently by the hands and pulled her to her feet. "How about I take you home?"

"What about the interment? I have to be there when, when—" Emma bit her lip, trying not to cry.

"You need to get out of those wet clothes. You can change at home, and then I'll drive you to the cemetery."

"Okay." Emma was glad to let Sam decide what to do; she couldn't think about anything except her mother right then.

Sam guided her through the parking lot filled with Mercedes and BMWs to a blue Ford pickup. He helped Emma up into the cab of the truck, then shut the door for her. He trotted around to the driver's side and got in, brushing his wet hair off his face.

"I'll turn the heater on for us," he said, and promptly did so.

Within minutes the cab was warm as toast; the welcome heat took the chill off Emma's drenched body. Her teeth stopped chattering and she even managed a small smile for Sam.

They drove in silence across town.

"It's the last house on the right," Emma said when they turned down Pleasanton Street.

"I remember," Sam said.

Emma was surprised. She couldn't recall ever inviting Sam over to her house. She had no idea where he lived.

Sam pulled up into the driveway and Emma got out. "You should get out of your wet clothes, too, you know," she told him.

"My house is only a couple of minutes away." Sam looked at her closely. "I could run home and change and then come back for you. But I don't want to leave you alone."

"I'm fine," Emma said. "Really. Please go."

"If you're sure it's okay ... "

Emma nodded.

Sam smiled. "I'll be right back, I promise."

Emma watched him drive off, then ran into the house and up to her room. She stripped off her dripping dress and dumped it into the tub, pushing it to the back. Then she stepped in and turned on the shower. As the hot water streamed over her she leaned her forehead against the cool tile and cried. She felt like crying forever, but she knew she couldn't, not yet. So she turned off the water and left the tub. Grabbing a towel, she rubbed her pale, freckled skin harshly. The pain felt good. She looked across the room at the bathroom mirror, which revealed red eyes and swollen lids. She looked terrible. Not that she cared.

She rubbed the towel over her long, wavy red hair. Heavy and wet, it would take too long to dry, even with her blow dryer, so she quickly twisted it into a French braid. She smoothed some moisturizer on her bare face and applied clear gloss to her lips. That would have to do.

As she slipped into a pair of jeans and a warm sweater, tears filled her eyes and she looked at her bed with longing. She hated the thought of the cemetery and of watching them bury her mother in the cold, dank ground. All she wanted to do was crawl into that bed and stay there until she stopped hurting, until she stopped missing her mother.

But Emma knew she must go; she owed her mother that much. The doorbell rang, and she realized Sam was waiting for her. She pulled on a pair of warm socks and her boots, grabbed her coat, and then walked downstairs with leaden feet and a heavy heart to meet him.

Without a word he ushered her into the cab of his truck and drove her in silence to the cemetery on the outskirts of town.

The rain had slowed to a relentless drizzle; a gray mist hung over the road like a shroud. At Sam's suggestion they parked outside the cemetery, so that they could leave early if they wanted to. Sam produced a black umbrella big enough for two and they walked quietly through the landscaped grounds of death. Even on such a dreary day it was a beautiful place, lined with stately oaks and ornamental hedges.

They made their way across the rolling hills of the cemetery to the tree-filled grove where six generations of Lambournes were buried. Tall marble headstones marked the graves: the first Lambourne to come to America from England, Oliver Lambourne, 1865–1923; Gertrude Harrington Lambourne, Oliver's beloved wife, 1875–1931; Grandmother Beatrice's husband, Charles Henry Lambourne, 1925–1985; Emma's father, Henry James Lambourne, 1948–1979.

Emma resisted an odd urge to kick the Lambournes' gravestones as she and Sam walked by. These people had never liked her mother; they'd never really accepted her. How cruel that she should have to lie with them for eternity. Emma bit her lip, trying to hold back the tears. Her mother wouldn't have wanted her to feel that way; after all, she would lie next to her husband, the only man she had ever loved.

There was a freshly dug open grave by her father's gravesite. A canopy had been set up; chairs for the bereaved, now as empty as the grave, waited for their arrival.

Emma looked away. She watched the long line of expensive cars follow the hearse as it wound through the cemetery, bringing her mother to her final resting place. She watched as the hearse stopped nearby and the pallbearers carried the coffin in under the canopy.

Friends and family emerged from their cars. Sally accompanied Grandmother Beatrice; she gave Emma a sympathetic look as they approached the canopy. All of Kenilworth was there; every one of her classmates from Kenilworth High had come, along with Emma's teachers. She was touched. The sight of their solemn young faces again brought tears to her eyes.

They gathered under the canopy, and the minister began his last words. Emma looked past the open grave to her father's massive marble headstone, which read *Beloved Husband and Father.* Blinking back more tears, she thought longingly of the father she'd never really known and the mother she would never see again.

Sam took her hand as her mother's coffin was lowered into the grave. Emma squeezed his hand tightly in return. Then she shut her eyes and prayed for her mother, prayed that wherever Grace Lambourne was, she was with her husband, Henry, and happy again.

And prayed for herself, too, that somehow she could survive without the one person who loved her most.

Sam accompanied Emma to Grandmother Beatrice's mansion, where the close friends and family of Grace Lambourne were gathering for refreshments after the funeral.

Emma's mother, Grace, had been a solitary person with no blood relations except her daughter. She had had few friends. Her world had revolved around her only child. It always had, Emma realized as she watched the people sampling her grandmother's afternoon buffet. Most of the guests were friends and family of Grandmother Beatrice; they were there because she expected them to be, not because they loved Grace.

Everyone seemed to be avoiding Emma. Oh, one by one they all came over to mumble their awkward condolences, but they didn't stay long. They said the proper thing and then darted for the buffet table. Even her young cousins avoided her, although they did sneak looks at her when the grown-ups weren't looking. Emma figured they were embarrassed for her after she'd made such a scene at the church. And now there she was in jeans at her dead mother's reception. They probably thought she was crazy, on the verge of a nervous breakdown or something. If you had a breakdown in Kenilworth, you were supposed to do it in the privacy of your own mansion—not in a public place and certainly not in church.

"Do *you* think I'm crazy?" Emma turned to Sam, who stood next to her holding a china plate of uneaten hors d'oeuvres.

"No."

"They all seem to."

"These people are weird," said Sam matter-of-factly. "Except for Sally."

"They're my family," Emma said, defending them.

"You'd never know it to look at them."

"What do you mean?"

"You've got class."

"You're not saying..." Emma stared at him. "But Grandmother Beatrice is the classiest woman in Kenilworth."

"If you say so." Sam's tone was dismissive. "Listen, you've had a long day. Why don't I take you home?"

Emma nodded. She would have liked nothing better than to go home to bed and stay there forever. "I have to say good-bye to my grandmother first."

"I'll go get the truck." Sam excused himself, and Emma went in search of Grandmother Beatrice. She was holding court in the enormous living room, talking to two of Emma's great-aunts.

"A terrible display," her grandmother was saying. "Emma is such an emotional girl. The genes will out, you know. I warned Henry when he married that woman—"

Emma shrank back. She didn't want to hear any more. She slipped out of the living room unnoticed, and left.

Sally stopped her on the way out. "Emma, what's wrong?"

Emma choked back tears. "Nothing, it's nothing."

Sally hugged Emma to her chest. "That old biddy said something, didn't she? Mean old witch ... Look, you just forget it. She's wrong, no matter what she said."

"Right." Emma hugged Sally tighter, then pulled away.

"Do you want me to take you home?"

"No, stay here and make my excuses. Sam will take me home."

Sally smiled. "Okay. You're in good hands with Sam. I'll drop by later and check up on you."

Sam was waiting for Emma in the pickup outside. When she got in, he apologized. "I shouldn't have said anything about your family. I was way out of line. You've been through enough today—I didn't mean to make it worse for you."

"You didn't." Emma looked at him thoughtfully. "You don't like them much, do you?"

Sam shook his head. "No," he said honestly. "I don't. But I like you."

"You would have liked my mother," Emma told him, her eyes filling with tears.

Sam drove her home then. He didn't say anything. She was grateful to him for understanding that she didn't feel like talking anymore. She was suddenly exhausted, physically and emotionally spent.

By the time he pulled into her driveway, Emma was half asleep. She allowed Sam to help her into the house, where she collapsed on the couch.

Without saying a word, he gently kissed her forehead. Then he covered her with an afghan and was gone. The touch of his lips on her skin pierced the thick veil of her grief, just for a moment. *What a wonderful guy,* she thought briefly before she fell back into the dark well of mourning and cried herself to sleep.

CHAPTER FOUR

Emma dreamed of owls—gray owls, screech owls, barn owls, tawny owls—circling the night of her mind, calling "Cu, *cu, cu!"* Feathers flying, the birds of prey searched the dark sky, looking, looking, looking. They soared and dipped and then suddenly dived. Shrieking like banshees, the owls closed in on her, their great wings banging against her limbs and their talons clawing her face. Her mother appeared, pale as death, wielding a great sword. The owls scattered. "Look for the owl," she wailed, swinging the sword around her head like a warrior. "Look for the owl."

Emma awoke with a start. She sat bolt upright, and found herself on her mother's overstuffed beige couch in the living room. It was very late; the house was dark and quiet. All Emma could hear was the pounding of the rain on the roof and the whistling of the wind through the eaves.

She switched on the crystal lamp by the couch. There she found a short note from Sally.

Em—

Didn't have the heart to wake you. I know you want to be alone, so I'm resisting the urge to stay here and watch over you. But you must call me the minute you wake up, no matter when that is. That means now.

Love,
Sally

Shivering, Emma pulled the afghan up around her shoulders. She wasn't up to talking to any Lambourne at the moment, not even Sally. She was still hurting from that nasty crack Grandmother Beatrice had made about her mother at the reception.

Emma leaned her head back against the soft tufted arm of the couch and closed her eyes. She saw her mother again, near death, whispering, "I can't leave you all alone. Look for the owl."

Look for the owl. In the terrible days since her mother's death, she had forgotten her mother's odd directive. At the time she had dismissed her mother's words, thinking she didn't know what she was saying. But now Emma wasn't so sure.

Look for the owl. What could it mean? Emma didn't remember ever seeing an owl around the house, real or otherwise. Was it a clue to something more, or did it refer to a real owl?

Emma stood up, deciding at that very moment to find the owl. But where should she look for it? Her mother had been a homebody, and the house had been her life.

Everything her mother had loved and valued was right there in her home. So it had to be in the house somewhere.

She searched systematically, beginning in the basement. There wasn't much that was mysterious down there. Shelving lined the concrete walls, displaying row upon row of the Ball jars her mother had used to can her homegrown fruit and vegetables—tomatoes, beets, pickles, peaches, plums, and her famous strawberry preserves. Emma found a couple of old boxes hidden in a dank corner, but all they held were more Ball jars. So much for the basement.

Emma went upstairs to the first floor, working her way slowly through the rooms. In the kitchen pantry she came across an entire set of china packed away behind the spice racks. She'd never seen it before. She held one of the fragile teacups in the palm of her hand. It was fine china, delicately painted in an old-fashioned style with pink roses and monogrammed with the initials *C & B L*—Charles and Beatrice Lambourne.

It was Grandmother Beatrice's china, obviously a gift her mother hadn't cared for. Now that she knew what her grandmother really thought of her mother, Emma could understand why. She put the cup back. The next day she'd wrap the china up and give it to Sally to return to her grandmother. If her mother hadn't wanted it, neither did she.

Emma checked out the dining room, but the antique hutch there revealed only her mother's collections of Victorian cut glass and lace linens. On to the living room. Her mother's desk was there, a simple but splendid

Queen Anne piece. This was where her mother had "kept her accounts"—her ladylike way of referring to paying the bills.

There were only two drawers in the desk: one filled with the usual insurance and tax files, the other containing staples, stamps, pens, pencils, and her mother's perfumed, engraved stationery. Emma lifted a sheet to her face, drinking in her mother's favorite scent—Chanel Number Five. Tears filled her eyes as she replaced the sheet in the drawer. Nothing there but the living spirit of her mother.

Emma made a cursory check of the downstairs bathroom and then continued upstairs. First she explored the two guest rooms, which featured virtually empty bureaus and closets. She bypassed her room altogether—she knew all too well what junk was in there.

And so she came to the one room she'd been avoiding: her mother's bedroom. It was a beautiful room, as beautiful as her mother. Grace had decorated it when she married Emma's father, and she'd changed nothing since the day he died. She'd left his highboy just as he'd left it, even down to the change in the brass dish that sat on the top of the dresser.

It was a room where time stood still. The elegant cream-and-white room was a soothing place, a feminine place, draped in silks and brocades and laces. Emma sat on the high four-poster bed, sinking into the rich down comforter. When she was a little girl, she would sneak into this room whenever she had had a bad dream and cuddle with her mother in this bed.

Part of her wanted to do just that once again—wrap herself in her mother's linens and wish the bad dream away. But she wasn't a little girl anymore; since her mother's death she felt far older than her seventeen years. She sighed and pushed herself to her feet. There were only two places to look: the armoire and the walk-in closet.

Carefully she searched the drawers of her mother's beloved antique French armoire. Lined with perfumed paper, the large drawers held the usual bras and panties, sweaters and socks, jeans and leggings. But the smaller drawers held the treasures of her mother's life: the pearls Emma's father had given her mother on their wedding day; the long satin gloves she had worn at her debutante's ball; a pressed rosebud from her bridal bouquet.

These were all souvenirs Emma had seen before. Still, she sobbed at the sight of them. Reaching behind the satin gloves in a deep corner of the top drawer, she felt something smooth and hard. She pulled out a small soapstone box, a simple square with a lift-off lid. She'd never seen it before; it looked like nothing else her mother owned. Curious, she lifted off the lid. Inside was fine old lace, yellowed with age but of obvious quality. Emma carefully unfolded the lace, and there it was. An odd arc of dull gold. She touched it, and received a small shock. Emma shrank back, as if the thing were dangerous. Absurd. She picked up the heavy gold piece and held it in her palm.

It was clearly something of value, for her mother had kept it all these years. She had no idea what it was, but she was certain of one thing: her search was over. This strange curve of gold tubing was what she was looking for. "Look for the owl," her mother had told her—and there it was. At least, part of one.

For one end of the gold arc flattened into a distinct shape: that of a single spread wing and one half of an eerie, wise-looking owl's head and body. From the strange split face sparkled a lone emerald eye. Emma stared at it, transfixed. An unexpected sense of foreboding overcame her. For some reason the odd warning of the old gypsy woman popped into her head: "The world as you know it is about to be turned upside down."

Emma had found the owl, and she knew—without knowing why—that her life would never be the same again.

"You never called me," chided Sally as she burst into Emma's house without knocking the next morning around nine.

Emma was in the kitchen making a pot of tea. "What are you doing here? Shouldn't you be in school?"

"It's Saturday." Sally gave her a hug. "Poor baby, you don't even know what day it is anymore."

Emma ignored her. "If it's Saturday, what are you doing up so early?" Sally rarely rose before noon on Saturdays, unless a particularly cute guy made it worth her while. But there she was, not only up but dressed as well—in a very expensive blue wool suit that matched her eyes. Sally always dressed as if she were chairwoman of the board rather than the high school student she really was.

"I've asked Jared Clarke to take us to the Chicago Museum of Modern Art. There's a new Ansel Adams exhibit there; I thought it might cheer you up."

"That explains the outfit."

Sally struck a sophisticated pose. "Very chic, don't you think?"

Emma nodded. "That's very sweet of you, Sally, but the Adams exhibit has been sold out for months." She waved Sally into a chair and poured them each a cup of tea.

Sally grinned. "I know, but Jared's been dying to go out with me for much longer than that."

Emma laughed in spite of herself. "You told him he could take you out if he got the tickets."

Sally shook her pretty blond head. "Of course not. I simply dropped a little hint about the exhibit, that's all." She leaned forward across the table. "You know, Emma, now that you've got Sam on the line, you have to learn not to be so direct if you're going to hook him."

"He's not a fish, Sally, and I'm not trying to hook him."

Sally sipped her tea. "He's a good catch, Emma. You don't want to scare him off like you have all the others, do you?"

Emma did not dignify that with a response. She drank her tea in silence.

"You like him," Sally insisted. "And he likes you. I saw the way he was looking at you yesterday. He's yours for the asking."

Emma sighed. "Okay, I admit it. I like him. But right now I really can't think about that." She stood up from the table. "Look, there's something I have to show you."

At that moment the doorbell rang.

"Jared?" Emma looked to Sally for confirmation.

"No," Sally said, "I told him to wait in the limo."

"The *limo*?" Emma rolled her eyes.

"I'll get the door. You run upstairs and put on some mascara." She looked at Emma with the critical eye of a cosmetologist. "And a little blush and lip gloss."

"Why?"

It was Sally's turn to roll her eyes. "Because it's Sam, you idiot."

"You don't know that," Emma said, but she did as she was told anyway. When it came to guys, there was no arguing with Sally. Guys were her main area of expertise; she knew men the way Emma knew photography. Emma had learned over time simply to bow to Sally's greater wisdom on this particular subject. Besides, she didn't have the strength to fight her just then.

So she went upstairs and dutifully brushed her hair, blushed her cheeks, and glossed her lips. She drew the line at mascara, which she felt looked unnatural. Finished, she looked in the mirror, wondering for the millionth time in her life why she had been born the only redhead in a sea of blond Lambournes. Her mother had always made her feel beautiful, but now that she was gone Emma saw herself as she really was—the black sheep, alone.

She turned away from the mirror. When she went back downstairs, she found Sally in her Kenilworth hostess mode, entertaining Sam in the living room.

"Emma." Sam stood up immediately to greet her. "How are you feeling?"

"Better, thanks. Please sit down." She joined him on the couch. "I'd like to show you both something." Emma looked at Sally. "Do you have the time?"

"Sure." Sally grinned. "Jared will wait."

"It won't take long." Emma withdrew the gold piece from the soapstone box on the coffee table, holding it out on her open palm for Sally and Sam to see.

"What is it?" asked Sam.

"I don't know." Emma had spent what was left of the previous night staring at it, trying to figure that out. "Any ideas, Sally?"

Sally regarded the gold piece with interest. "May I?" she asked.

Emma nodded her consent.

Sally took the gold piece from Emma's hand and examined it. "I don't know, but whatever it is, it's expensive. It feels like real gold, and that looks like a genuine emerald eye to me." She handed the piece to Sam. "Your turn," she said to him, then addressed Emma. "Where did you get it?"

"It was my mother's." Emma told them about her mother's strange last instructions.

Sam examined it closely. "It must be a piece of jewelry. But how would you wear it?"

"Exactly." Emma nodded, glad she could share her mysterious discovery. "It's too small to be a bracelet."

Sam held the gold piece up to his ear. He twisted his neck to show it off, as if he were a fashion model.

Sally and Emma laughed.

"Too big to be an earring," said Sally.

Sam laughed with them, then placed the gold oddity in Emma's open hand and curled her slender fingers up around it. "You should take it to a jeweler. Maybe they can tell you what it is."

"I bet Grandmother Beatrice knows. She knows everything that goes on in this family."

Sam squeezed her hand, then released it. "Maybe. But even if she knows, she may not tell you. I get the feeling she tells people only what she thinks they should know."

"You think she'd lie to me?" Emma had never thought her grandmother capable of lying, for all her faults. It was more like her to tell the truth, no matter how much it hurt people.

Sally answered that for him. "I don't know. She's usually brutally honest, but I'm sure she's capable of lying when it suits her."

Emma wrapped the gold piece in the old lace and put it back in the soapstone box. "I'll see her this afternoon when I go to the lawyer's office for the reading of the will. I can ask her about this owl thing afterward."

"Do you want me to come with you?" asked Sally and Sam in unison.

Emma smiled at them both. "No, thanks. This is something I have to do on my own."

Sam hesitated. "Okay. Just promise me you'll take whatever your grandmother says with a grain of salt."

"Ditto," said Sally.

Emma was touched by their obvious concern for her. "I promise."

"When are you due at the lawyers?" asked Sally.

"Three o'clock."

"I'll switch the tickets for a better day," said Sally. "Maybe next weekend."

"I'm sorry, Sally," Emma said.

"No problem. I can see you're really not up to it yet anyway." Sally stood to go. "I'd better go. I've been keeping Jared waiting long enough." She turned to Sam. "I'm leaving her in your capable hands, Sam Tyler. Take good care of her."

"I will."

Over Emma's protests, Sam made her a late breakfast.

"This looks delicious," Emma said as he placed a platter with a Spanish omelette and home fries in front of her. "I'm hungrier than I thought."

"I'm not surprised. You haven't eaten much lately."

"I guess not. I've been too upset to eat."

"I understand. But you do need to keep up your strength." He grinned. "I'll be glad to cook for you anytime."

Emma blushed. She wasn't used to such attention from a guy. "Thanks," she said. "I'll be a good girl and clean my plate."

"Thank you," he said, watching her with affection as she finished her meal. "Now, time for a nap."

"A nap?"

"You haven't gotten much sleep lately, either, have you?"

"No," admitted Emma. The truth was, she needed to be at her most alert that afternoon at the lawyer's. A nap would probably do her some good.

"Go ahead. I can amuse myself."

Emma looked at him. "You don't have to stay."

"I'd like to stay, if you don't mind." Sam leaned across the table toward her with that sweet, sincere look of his.

Emma felt an overwhelming urge to kiss him. She stared down at her lap. "I don't mind."

"Great." Sam reached over and took her plate. "You go on upstairs and I'll clean up down here. When shall I wake you?"

The thought of Sam in her bedroom unnerved her. "Oh, don't worry," she said, "I'll set the alarm."

And then she bolted upstairs, before Sam could see her blushing again.

By three in the afternoon the rain had stopped and the sun shone in a clear blue sky. Emma's dreamless nap had refreshed her somewhat, but the prospect of hearing the will read had once again brought home the pain of her mother's death. Numb with grief, she slipped into a navy silk shirtdress and matching low-heeled shoes; with trembling hands she fastened the pearl necklace her mother had given her on her sixteenth birthday around her neck. She looked in the mirror; a sad-eyed young woman stared back at her.

She came downstairs and told Sam to go home.

"I really need to be alone for a while," she said, looking into his kind, honest eyes. Instinctively, she reached up and touched his cheek. "I can't thank you enough for all ... " Her voice faltered.

Sam closed his hand over hers. "You don't have to thank me." He squeezed her hand, then released it. "I'll call you after supper."

He left then, and Emma was alone again.

CHAPTER FIVE

With a heavy heart Emma drove her mother's beige BMW to Mr. Goldsmith's office. Mr. Goldsmith was an old friend of her father's, and he'd served as the best man at her parents' wedding. Her mother had trusted him, so Emma did, too.

Grandmother Beatrice was there waiting for her when she pulled into the parking lot. Emma got out of the car and started toward the antique black Daimler. Her grandmother watched her approach; Emma saw her tap her gold-tipped cane on the window—her signal to the chauffeur to open the door for her.

Charlie, looking spiffy as always in his black uniform, graciously helped the proud old lady out of her plush vehicle.

"Hi, Charlie," Emma said, managing a small smile. She liked Charlie; he still sneaked her peppermints when Grandmother Beatrice wasn't looking, just as he had when she was a little girl.

"Emma," her grandmother said sternly. "Don't dawdle."

Her grandmother did not approve of making small talk with the servants. Emma turned to her grandmother with a solemn air. "I'm ready."

She went to take her grandmother's arm, but the old lady shook her off. Emma shrugged, and followed her grandmother as she made her way slowly with her cane into the nondescript brown professional building. They took the elevator to the second floor, where Grandmother Beatrice led her to suite 231, home of the law firm Goldsmith and Laraby.

Emma had been there before, accompanying her mother when she went for a consultation. But despite the familiarity of the book-lined office, Emma panicked. She saw herself finally as the orphan she was—alone, and dependent solely upon whatever her mother had left of her father's estate.

Mr. Goldsmith sat behind a long oak desk covered with a sheet of glass. He was a small man, neat and dapper in his blue serge suit. He had a round head with very little hair. His brown eyes were kind under the expanse of hairless scalp. He sat very still in the high-backed chair, as if in silent remembrance of Emma's mother. He motioned to Emma and her grandmother to take their seats in the tufted black leather chairs that faced his desk. They sat in silence and waited, Grandmother Beatrice tapping her cane in impatience.

Finally Mr. Goldsmith spoke. His voice was soft and deep. "I have your mother's will and testament before me, Emma. Of course, she leaves everything to you. I'll read it for you, as a good lawyer should, even if it means very little to you."

And so Mr. Goldsmith began to read in his resonant voice. He was right. Emma understood little of it. After a while she stopped trying. She simply stared at Mr. Goldsmith to keep from crying, focusing on the spot where the light from the high window behind the desk hit his bald head. She had no idea how much time passed, but at last Mr. Goldsmith finished his recitation. He placed the papers on the desk before him, rapped his small fingers on the glass top, then sat back in his chair.

Grandmother Beatrice leaned forward on her cane. "So Emma gets everything. That's clear. But what is everything, exactly?"

Despite her harsh words the day before, Emma was grateful for her grandmother's presence; she could count on her to ask the terrible questions she couldn't.

Mr. Goldsmith placed his hands together so that they touched only at the fingertips. He seemed to study them for a moment, then lowered them to his lap abruptly. He rose to his feet and walked over to Emma. He squeezed her shoulder, then backed up to his desk and leaned against it. Facing them, he said, "Everything is not as much as it could be, Mrs. Lambourne. But it should bring enough to see Emma through college to self-sufficiency. And, of course, the house is hers outright." Mr. Goldsmith turned to Emma. "You always have the option to sell. It's a fine house in a fine neighborhood; it should bring a good price."

Emma reddened. "I could never sell my mother's house."

Grandmother Beatrice frowned. “Grace never was very good with money. She insisted on remaining in that big house, and indulging Emma in that expensive photographic hobby of hers. Any sensible person would have left the child more.”

As she listened to her grandmother a terrible rage filled Emma's heart. She wanted to yell at her, scream at her, even strike her. But she didn't. Her mother would not have approved; for her mother's sake and in her mother's name, Emma would act like a lady. Even when her grandmother did not.

Mr. Goldsmith cleared his throat with authority. “As a Lambourne, I'm sure Emma will never want for anything.”

“Grace counted on that, I'm sure.” Grandmother Beatrice stood up. “If there's nothing else, we'll be on our way.”

“Wait. I have something to show you.” Emma pulled the gold owl piece out of her purse. “Have you ever seen this before?”

Her grandmother blinked, then waved her hand dismissively and began to make her slow exit out of the office, cane in hand.

Emma looked at Mr. Goldsmith.

“No, Emma, I haven't. What is it?”

“I don't know, but I'm going to find out.” She thanked Mr. Goldsmith and raced after her grandmother. She caught up with her at the elevator. “Grandmother, I need to talk to you.”

Grandmother Beatrice gave her a shrewd look. "About money?"

"What?" Emma shook her head. "No, no. I want to talk to you about this gold piece. I know you know more than you're saying."

The elevator doors opened and the old lady strode out, cane tapping. Emma followed along behind her.

"Come to the house," her grandmother ordered as Charlie ushered her into the Daimler. "I can give you half an hour."

Emma waited for her grandmother in the library of the mansion, remembering the last time she had been there and what she had overheard. She held the gold piece tightly in her hand.

Her grandmother entered the room and walked with imperious grace to her chair, a brocade Louis XVI chair she permitted no one else to use. She eased herself into the chair with the help of her cane, then sat straight-backed and addressed Emma. "What do you want to know?"

Emma approached her grandmother with apprehension; suddenly she was not sure she wanted to know the truth the owl had to tell her.

Grandmother Beatrice took the gold piece from Emma's open palm.

"What is it?"

Her grandmother glanced at the object she held in her wrinkled fingers and then returned it to Emma. "I have no idea."

Emma wavered between disappointment and relief. *I guess Grandmother Beatrice doesn't know everything after all,* she thought with little satisfaction.

"I have something to tell you, something important," the old lady said, interrupting Emma's thoughts.

"Go ahead." Emma did not know what she was talking about, but the way she said "something important" chilled her.

Characteristically, Beatrice did not mince any words. "You are not really a Lambourne. You are adopted."

Emma stared at her. "I don't understand."

"It's really quite simple, Emma. Your mother was barren and could not have children of her own. My dear son loved her still, and married her anyway."

"You didn't approve." Emma fairly spat out the words.

"I approved of neither the marriage nor your adoption," said Grandmother Beatrice in a bitter tone. "But my son was stubborn, much like his father had been at that age. He agreed to adopt you, despite my misgivings."

"Misgivings?"

The old lady sighed. "Ours is a distinguished family. Bloodlines are so important, and—"

"And you didn't know where I came from."

"Your parents simply came home with you one day." She sniffed.

"But how—"

"Some ridiculous story about a poor gypsy girl," Grandmother Beatrice interrupted. "You were clearly illegitimate." Her tone communicated her disgust.

"That's why you've never liked me," Emma said with sudden insight.

Beatrice said nothing; her silence said it all.

Emma reeled with the secret knowledge of her birth, but still she pressed for more. "Did they tell you anything about where I came from, anything at all?"

"Your mother said your given name was Emerald. That's why she christened you Emma, so you wouldn't have to get used to a completely new name. Such non-sense, you were only a few days old at the time."

"Why didn't she tell me the truth?"

Grandmother Beatrice frowned. "Your mother was never a strong woman—physically or emotionally. After your father died, you were all she had left. I suppose she was afraid of losing you."

Emma wrapped the owl piece back up in the lace and returned it to the box. "Why didn't you like her? She was so kind and good and—"

"She wasn't good enough for my son," Grandmother Beatrice said stiffly.

And you think I'm not good enough for you, either, Emma thought. She rose to go, willing herself not to cry until she was safely gone from this terrible woman's house.

Without a word, Emma turned her back on her Grandmother Beatrice and walked out, her words ringing in her ears.

You aren't really a Lambourne.

You aren't really a Lambourne.

You aren't really a Lambourne.

Alone in her mother's house, Emma pored over the family album, looking for a sign—the shape of a nose, the rise of a cheekbone, the jut of a chin. She found nothing—not a single physical attribute she could claim from either her mother's or her father's family.

When she was a little girl, she had hated her red hair. She had asked her mother why she was the only one in the family with red hair.

"Oh, but you're not," her mother had told her. "My great-aunt Frieda had beautiful red hair just like yours." She showed Emma a picture of Frieda, the same one that Emma stared at now in the family album.

As a child Emma had been happy to link her red-haired destiny with the glamorous Frieda, who in the photo was striking a sophisticated pose as she was crowned Miss Winnetka 1928. But now Emma saw the faded black-and-white photo as the ultimate deceiver; for once her beloved black-and-white photography failed to tell her the truth about Frieda, her mother, herself.

Her mother had loved her and indulged her; Emma knew that. So why keep the adoption a secret? Why the elaborate pretense, why the telltale charade of Frieda?

Her mother must have done it for Emma's sake. So she could grow up like any other Kenilworth girl, spared the terrible knowledge that she was simply not as blue-blooded as the rest of them.

But *they* knew. Grandmother Beatrice and the rest of them, they had always known. Emma slammed the family album shut.

It explained so much: the feeling that she didn't really belong, the realization that not only did she not look like a Lambourne, she didn't act like one, either.

They had known all along, and they secretly hated her for it. Hated her for pretending to be a Lambourne, for being the imposter.

Her mother might have succeeded in protecting her from the truth, but she couldn't protect her from their hatred. Emma's eyes filled with tears. How her mother must have suffered, knowing she had failed to give her daughter the one thing she needed most: a family.

"I can't leave you all alone," she had told Emma before she died.

But she had, she had left her all alone. Emma was suddenly possessed of an uncharacteristic anger, an anger that raged at the bittersweet memory of the kind woman who had raised her. The kind woman who was *not* her mother.

The tears came then—bitter tears Emma promised herself would be the last she shed for the Lambournes. After a while she got up and put the family album away in a dark corner of a rarely used closet, where she would be unlikely to come across it.

Then she slowly toured the house, turning to the wall all of the photographic portraits she'd so lovingly taken of her mother. She couldn't bear to see her mother's smiling face. Not at that moment. Maybe not ever.

It hurt too much.

Chapter Six

The next weeks were interminable. Sally showed up every morning promptly at seven-thirty to drag her out of bed and into the shower, so Emma continued to go to school.

Sally believed it was important that Emma graduate along with the rest of her class. Emma couldn't have cared less whether she received a Kenilworth High School diploma or not. But Sally was her best friend and the only family she had left. The rest of the Lambournes had fallen in line behind the formidable Grandmother Beatrice; only Sally had the courage and the clout to defy her.

"I don't care what anybody says," Sally told Emma over and over again. "As far as I'm concerned, you're family. You're as much a Lambourne as I am."

If Sally could suffer the wrath of Beatrice, Emma could suffer through the last days of high school—what Sally insisted was the best time of their lives.

So she went through the motions, accompanying Sally to the graduation planning meetings, the rallies, the yearbook committee meetings, and the student debates. As the official class photographer, Emma also attended the endless round of lunches and dances and parties, shooting for posterity all of her fellow classmates having fun, fun, fun while she just wanted to go home, home, home.

The only time she really had any fun was with Sam. Sam had come up from the city every weekend without fail since her mother's death. He'd stay at his folks' house and check in on her often, bringing her flowers and chocolate and photography magazines. Sensing her need for solitude, he never overstayed his welcome.

As time went on these visits became more like dates, thanks to Sally's relentless matchmaking. More often than not they double-dated with Sally and her latest guy, indulging Sally's latest impulse—from museum exhibits to fancy uptown soirées. What Emma still liked best, however, were those quiet nights at home with Sam, watching videos and ordering in pizza. She sometimes wished he would give her more than a kiss on the cheek when he left, but in truth she knew she probably couldn't handle much more than that for a while.

"Sally says you refuse to go to the prom," Sam said to her on one such Saturday night as they sat in front of the TV watching HBO.

Emma frowned. "I'm supposed to take the pictures, but..." Her voice trailed off. "I don't know, I just don't feel up to all the hoopla."

"It's been a couple of months now, Emma," Sam said gently. "I know you need to grieve, but you also need to get on with your life. Your mother would want that, you know."

Emma knew he was right, but how could she get on with her life if she didn't know who she was? She'd never told Sam about the adoption; she was too ashamed. Only Sally knew, and the rest of the Lambournes, of course, all of whom Emma avoided as assiduously as they avoided her. "I don't know."

"I didn't go to my senior prom," Sam said.

"Why not?" asked Emma.

"Because I didn't have the guts to ask the girl I wanted to go with. I've regretted it ever since."

Before Emma could respond Sam pulled her to him and kissed her hard, full on the lips. No one had ever kissed Emma like that before; she felt her very breath drain away.

Sam released her abruptly. "In case you haven't guessed, you are that girl."

"Oh, Sam," Emma said, "I'm so sorry. I had no idea."

"Make it up to me by taking me to your prom." He held out his arms to her. Emma fell into them. "Why not?" she whispered. He closed his strong arms around her and pressed her to his chest. He kissed her again, and this time she kissed him back.

"What are you going to wear?" Sally asked her when Emma told her about Sam and the prom. They were in the kitchen, making chocolate chip cookies.

"My red silk jumpsuit." Emma was mixing the dough with a thick wooden spoon.

"You're not serious." Sally handed her a measuring cup full of chocolate chips.

"Sally, I have to take pictures. I need to wear something practical." Emma poured in the chips and mixed some more.

"No, you don't. Ken Walden is going to take them." Sally took the bowl from Emma. She placed it on the counter before her and began shaping little balls of dough, which she then handed to Emma to place on the cookie sheet. Sally and Emma had been making cookies together since they were little girls; they had it down to a delicious science. The trick was to eat as much of the dough as they baked.

"What are you talking about?" Emma popped one of the dough balls into her mouth. "That's my job as class photographer."

"He's a good photographer," mumbled Sally, her mouth full of chocolate chips.

"He's a sophomore."

"Exactly." Sally threw a dough ball at Emma. "This is the senior prom. Seniors are supposed to have fun—not work."

Emma caught it and tossed it back. "But it's my job."

Sally opened her mouth and caught the dough ball with her teeth. "Not anymore it's not," she said as soon as she could talk. "Emma, you hide behind that camera. You don't want to be an observer all your life, do you? That's what your mother did and—" Sally stopped short. "Oh, Emma, I'm so sorry, I—"

"It's all right." Emma regarded her friend with amazement. Sally obviously knew as much about women as she did about men. She understood people instinctively, intuitively; she didn't have to capture people on film to study them. "You're right. When Daddy died, she withdrew from the world. And she took me with her."

Sally hugged Emma. "I want you to participate in life. With me. With Sam. With all of us." To Emma's surprise, Sally had tears in her eyes. "We need you, Emma. You're such a beautiful, wonderful person."

"Okay, I'll participate, I promise." Emma hugged Sally back. "Ken can take the pictures, and you can take me shopping for a dress. Now get over there and finish those dough balls."

Sally smiled through her tears. "I've been so afraid that you would disappear into this house and never come out again. Especially to see me."

Emma was stunned. "Why would I do that?"

"Because I'm a Lambourne. After all that's happened, I wouldn't blame you if you never spoke to any of us again."

Emma laughed. "I can't believe this. I've been worried that you're going to give in to family pressure and dump me."

Sally laughed, too, scooping up a handful of chocolate chip cookie dough and throwing it at Emma. It landed in Emma's long red hair. Emma giggled, and grabbed her own handful of dough. She tossed it at Sally's ample chest, and collapsed in giggles when the pieces of dough fell into Sally's cleavage. The food fight was on. Emma and Sally whooped and giggled as the dough flew.

"You look beautiful," Sam told her when he picked her up on prom night.

"Thank you," Emma said, suddenly shy. As promised, Emma had let Sally pick out a dress for her. The strapless emerald satin gown was much too glamorous for Emma, who felt most comfortable in her usual uniform of jeans, T-shirt, and her trusty photographer's vest. But still she felt surprisingly pretty, in spite of herself.

Sam presented her with an artful bouquet of cream-colored roses and baby's breath, trimmed in emerald ribbon that matched her gown perfectly.

"How did you know—" Emma stopped. It had to have been Sally.

"Sally," they said in unison, and laughed.

The tension broken, Emma took Sam's arm easily and off they went into the night. They dined by candlelight at Kenilworth's best French restaurant, and danced every dance at the Kenilworth Country Club, where the ritzy affair was being held. With Sam holding her in his arms as the band played the last song, Emma allowed herself to feel happy. She rested her head on his shoulder as they danced, and thought only of Sam and how much she loved being with him.

But she couldn't hold on to her happiness. After the country club closed its doors, Sally's date, Tom, invited them to a post-prom bash at a large estate outside of town. Emma dozed off as Sam drove; when they pulled up in front of the neo-Georgian mansion, Emma awoke. She looked at the mansion and her heart ached.

"I can't go in there," she told Sam.

"Why not?" Sam grinned at her. "Not good enough for you?"

"I'm afraid it's the other way around," Emma said softly.

"What do you mean?"

"That's my cousin's house," Emma said pointedly. "James Garrett Lambourne the third."

"I don't understand."

"It's a long story." Emma looked away. "I'd like to go home now, if you don't mind."

"But—"

"Please," Emma said, hearing the whimper that had crept into her voice and hating herself for it.

"No problem." Sam turned the pickup around and headed back up the long, winding road that led to the estate. "I like the looks of your house better, anyway."

Why does he have to be so nice? Emma thought with chagrin. *It would be so much easier if he just weren't so nice.* To her own surprise she burst into tears.

Tires screeching, Sam abruptly pulled over to the side of the road. Without saying a word, he gathered Emma in his arms and held her as she sobbed. Emma cried for a long time.

When her tears subsided, Sam wiped her wet cheeks with his strong fingers. "I want you to tell me the whole story, start to finish. And don't leave anything out."

Emma shivered. Sam wrapped his tuxedo jacket around her shoulders.

"Talk," he ordered.

Emma talked. The entire terrible truth poured out of her—her grandmother, her mother's great-aunt Frieda, her adoption. As Sam had instructed, she left nothing out. It took a long time, and it hurt her to tell it. She thought she'd die telling it. But when she finished, finally, she felt nearly alive again.

"I don't know who I am," she said to Sam in a quiet voice. "I'm nobody."

"That's ridiculous." Sam lifted her chin gently, staring at her with stern blue eyes. "Listen to me. You're the same wonderful girl you were yesterday."

Emma smiled at him sadly. "You don't understand. You *can't* understand." She reached up and pushed the rearview mirror toward Sam. "You look in the mirror and you see your heritage staring back at you—your father's eyes, your mother's chin, your grandmother's nose, your grandfather's hair."

She pulled the mirror back toward her own face and stared into it. "When I look in the mirror, I see nothing but lies. Everything I knew about myself, everything I believed about myself—it's all lies."

"It doesn't matter, Emma. Nobody cares where you came from."

"The Lambournes care."

Sam frowned. "The Lambournes are a bunch of moronic snobs."

Emma shook her head. "Maybe. But I care, too. I care where I came from." She slapped the mirror up toward the roof of the truck. "I don't know who I am anymore."

"You can be anybody you want to be. You just need to put this behind you and get on with your life."

"I can't. How can I know where I'm going when I don't know where I came from?"

Sam sighed. "You're obsessed."

"I can't help it. It's just the way I feel."

"Okay." Sam wrapped his arms around her, then leaned over and kissed the top of her head. "So when do we start?"

Emma lifted her face to Sam's and allowed him to kiss her softly on the lips. "Start what?" she murmured.

Sam kissed her again. "Finding out who you really are," he answered as he drew her to him. "What else?"

"I don't understand it, Sam," Emma said. "We haven't found out a single thing." She sat with Sam on the couch in the living room, eating popcorn and watching HBO. They'd spent the past week trying to find out who Emma's biological parents were. This was the first time since the prom they'd just hung out together at home, doing nothing.

"We've looked everywhere," Sam admitted. "I've hacked into all the databases that apply. There's nowhere left to look." He grabbed another handful of popcorn.

Emma wasn't interested in popcorn. She jumped to her feet and began roaming the room restlessly, absently picking things up from tables and bookshelves and replacing them without really noticing them. "We must have missed something."

"I can't imagine what."

"Let's go over it one more time."

"Emma, don't torture yourself—"

"Please."

Sam sighed and flicked off the TV with the remote. "Okay. One more time—but that's it. Then we cuddle."

Emma smiled. "Deal. You start."

Sam leaned back on the couch, his hands folded behind his head. "We've consulted the birth records."

"And the adoption records."

"We've talked to Goldsmith, the lawyer. We've talked to your family members."

"You mean Sally talked to them."

"Right. Sally talked to them." Sam paused. "And we talked to the minister who baptized you."

Emma sighed. "And nobody knows anything."

"We've reached an impasse, that's all. We'll keep on trying. Somebody may remember something, we may think of a new database to break into—or maybe your biological parents will come looking for you at ARN."

ARN was the Adoptive's Rights Now dedicated to helping adopted children find their biological parents. Emma and Sam had visited their Chicago office, but hadn't found any clues to Emma's identity. ARN was keeping Emma's information on file, however, in case her biological parents should seek her out. "They haven't so far. Why would they change their minds?"

"They may be waiting for you to grow up."

"I'll be eighteen next week."

"Then give it a rest till next week." Sam patted the couch cushions. "Now come and sit down. You're missing some major cuddling here."

Emma laughed and went back to the couch. She sat next to Sam, but she couldn't relax. Sam sighed and switched the TV back on.

Emma leaned forward and took the soapstone box from the coffee table, where she'd placed it after that awful last encounter with her grandmother. Lifting off the top, she reached inside and removed the gold piece.

She fingered it tenderly. Despite her contradictory feelings about her adoption, Emma still loved the woman who had raised her—and this was her last tie to her.

"I can't leave you alone," her mother had said. "Look for the owl."

The green eye of the split owl stared at her like a wise Cyclops. Emma drew in her breath sharply. The owl had something to do with the mystery of Emma's identity—it must.

"It's a clue," Emma said with excitement.

"What are you talking about?" asked Sam, his eyes on the TV.

Emma waved the owl piece in front of Sam's face. "It's a clue. My mother was leaving me a clue to my identity. I can't believe we missed it." She stood up, then pulled Sam to his feet. "Come on," she said.

"Where are we going?" asked Sam good-naturedly.

"To check this out. If we can find out what this owl really is, we'll find out who I really am."

CHAPTER SEVEN

"Where did you get it?" the jeweler asked casually as he raised the loupe to his eye.

Emma and Sam stood at the counter of Martin's Jewelry, a small but distinguished shop in the heart of Victoria Place in Kenilworth. This small enclave of pricey boutiques housed in faux-Victorian gingerbread storefronts had been Emma's mother's favorite shopping area.

"My mother gave it to me," Emma said. In a way, it was true.

"I went to school with Grace," Hugh Martin told Emma as he examined the stone. "I was so sorry to hear of her death."

Emma nodded, unable to speak. She thought she would eventually get used to people talking about her mother's untimely death like that; in the weeks after her death it seemed to be all people talked about. She knew they meant well, and she was glad they hadn't forgotten her mother, but still, she found it hard to respond without getting teary. So mostly she just nodded and let them go on about her mother. It seemed to make them feel better.

"She was so beautiful and so young," Mr. Martin continued. "Much too young."

Emma nodded again. Behind her she heard the bell on the shop door jingle, signaling the arrival of another customer. Mr. Martin paid no attention to the newcomer.

"Such a terrible tragedy," he went on, removing the magnifying glass from his eye and regarding Emma gravely. "This must be a very difficult time for you."

Emma held back her tears. "Yes, it is," she managed to say.

"About the owl," Sam said, changing the subject, much to Emma's relief.

"It's very unusual. Do you have any idea how your mother came to have it?"

"No," answered Emma, more sharply than she intended.

Mr. Martin cast her an odd look. With his short, stout body and piercing gray eyes, he sort of looked like an owl himself. A cunning old owl.

"I mean, as far as I know, she always had it."

"I see." Mr. Martin placed the magnifying glass on the counter. He held the owl gold piece in his open palm. "All I can tell you is that it's unlike anything I've seen before. It's without a doubt twenty-four-karat gold. Not solid gold; it's plated onto metal tubing of some sort." He closed his fingers around the piece as if he meant to keep it. "I'd be glad to check into it for you."

Emma held out her hand for the gold piece. "Well ... "

"No charge, of course." Mr. Martin smiled at her for the first time. "As a favor to you and your poor mother."

"That's very generous of you, Mr. Martin, but—"

"Of course, I'll have to hold on to it for a while."

"Oh, I couldn't let you keep it," Emma said, reaching for the owl.

"Just for a little while. So I can show it around to experts, that sort of thing." Mr. Martin pulled his hand in toward his chest.

Emma was nonplussed. "But—"

Sam reached over and gripped Mr. Martin's wrist. "Mr. Martin, Emma would like her owl back now." Sam released his grip as quickly as he had secured it. Mr. Martin handed the owl over to Emma.

Sam put his arm around Emma protectively and turned her toward the door.

"Thank you for your time, Mr. Martin. We'll be in touch," he said over his shoulder as he hustled Emma out of the shop.

As soon as the door shut behind them Emma turned to Sam. "That wasn't like you, Sam. Why did you do that?"

"He wasn't going to give you the owl back." Sam hurried her across the parking lot.

"How do you know that?"

"He was lying."

"About what?"

"About the owl." Sam ushered her into his truck. "Come on, let's get out of here."

Emma snapped on her seat belt as Sam squealed out of the parking lot. "But he didn't say anything about it at all."

"Right. He knew more than he was saying."

Emma stared at Sam. "What do you mean?"

Sam's blue eyes darkened. "I think he knew exactly what it was, but he wouldn't tell us."

"Why not?"

Sam pulled over onto the shoulder of the road. He took her gently by the shoulders. "Your owl must be worth a lot of money, Emma. The way he looked at it... he wanted it for himself. That other guy seemed pretty interested, too."

"You mean the customer?"

"Yeah."

"I didn't notice him." But she had seen Mr. Martin. She framed in her mind the picture of the jeweler examining the gold piece. Beneath the jeweler's casual stance had been a tension—the tension of greed. "You're right. We can't take it back to him." She sighed at the thought of yet another dead end. At this rate she'd never find out who she was. "Now what?"

Sam took her by the hand. "Now we find out why Martin wanted the owl."

Professor Herman's office consisted of a desk, a phone, a computer, and hundreds—if not thousands—of books. Stacked neatly spine to spine, the books rose in tall columns against the walls. Most of the stacks climbed to the high ceiling of the small room, located in one of the older buildings on the University of Chicago campus. The Art History building, as Emma found out. Sam had brought her there to see this odd man Herman, who he claimed was a genius.

"He has an encyclopedic mind," Sam had told her on the commuter train on the way in. "If he doesn't know what it is, he'll know who to ask."

Now, sitting in his office on a pile of thick art volumes, Emma regarded the professor with skepticism. He was a small man with a large bald head fringed with gray curls. He wore bifocal glasses, which he continually adjusted with one tiny, restless hand as he caressed the owl piece with the other. He didn't look all that sane—much less smart—to her.

"What do you think, Professor Herman?" Sam asked.

"Quite unusual, Tyler." He motioned to Emma with a crook of a slender finger. She leaned forward toward the desk, and he deposited the gold piece carefully in her open palm. "You hold that, my dear, while I consult the authorities." With that he leapt from his chair and scampered among the stacks of books like a leprechaun frolicking in the forest.

Emma smiled, and cursed herself for not bringing her camera along. Sam had warned her against it, saying that the professor hated having his picture taken. "He thinks those primitive people who believe that photographers steal your soul when they take a picture of you are right," Sam had told her, laughing.

Emma had looked forward to meeting this eccentric man. She took pictures to reveal the world to herself—and to the people in it. Now that she'd met him, and liked him, she decided that maybe the professor was right: maybe the photographer could steal a person's soul—or at least reveal a little of it.

Professor Herman continued his dance among the books, plucking various volumes from their respective columns and stacking them neatly on his desk. He seemed to know where every book he needed was; there was a method to his madness, after all. Emma relaxed a bit, and for the first time she dared hope this funny little man could help her identify the owl.

His frolic finished, the professor returned to his desk. She and Sam sat quietly as he consulted the books set before him. Ten, twenty, thirty minutes passed in silence. Completely absorbed in his work, the professor seemed to forget they were there.

Another half an hour ticked by. Emma was getting hungry; it was nearly suppertime. She looked over at Sam, who winked at her. During all this waiting he had shown no hint of impatience. Emma wondered if he was naturally that patient or if it was a virtue he had acquired by taking college classes from the likes of Professor Herman.

More time passed. Emma's hunger died, replaced by an overwhelming sleepiness. Just as she was about to doze off, the professor lifted his large head from his scholarly work and grinned at them. He stabbed the open volume in front of him. "Victory, Tyler!"

Sam grabbed Emma's hand and pulled her over to the desk. She looked down to the place on the page marked by the professor's tiny index finger. A large photograph covered most of the page, revealing a beautiful gold and silver pin, richly decorated and studded with jewels.

"The patterns match," Emma said, amazed. "What is it?"

"It's the Irish Tara brooch," answered the professor. "A famous piece from the Celtic tradition, dating to around A.D. 800."

"A.D. 800?" Emma spluttered. "But that's over a thousand years ago. Are you saying that—"

"I don't know," interrupted the professor. "But I have an idea. Now that we've made the Celtic connection ... " His voice trailed off as he slammed the book on the Irish Tara brooch and pulled over another, equally thick volume. He flipped through the pages, a man with a mission. Again, Emma thought longingly of her camera.

"Here," said the professor, triumphant.

"Wow," said Sam.

"Wow," echoed Emma.

For there on the page in glorious color was her owl gold piece, only bigger and—more important—whole.

"It's the Blathnait torque," said the professor. "A classic tubular necklace of the Celts, dating from the first century B.C." The professor pointed to a smaller photo inset at the bottom of the page. The photograph revealed the torque as two pieces, two halves that together created a whole. Each half bore an owl split down the middle and sporting one emerald eye—just like Emma's split owl. Emma placed her gold piece next to the image of one half of the Blathnait necklace. The resemblance was overwhelming.

"The two gold pieces twist together to form the complete necklace," said the professor. Carefully he picked up the owl gold piece and held it up to the light. "What we have here appears to be one half of a Celtic torque."

"But it's so much smaller," said Sam.

Professor Herman turned the page, where a photo spread showed a variety of Celtic torques: necklaces, bracelets, ankle rings.

"It's half of a bracelet," said Emma. The relief of understanding flooded her. She leaned across the desk and kissed the odd man's bald head. "Thank you, Professor."

He giggled. "Now, my dear, I can't say for sure how much it's worth until I run some tests."

Emma grinned. "I don't care what it's worth. I just care whether it can tell me who I am."

"What do you mean?" The professor looked to Sam for explanation.

"Emma was reluctant to tell you the whole story."

"Let me explain," said Emma. She told him everything, from her mother's death to the trip to Martin's Jewelry. "I thought I was out of clues. But from what you tell me, I know where to look next." Emma smiled. "Ireland."

"Wait a minute," said Sam. "You're saying you're going to Ireland to check this out?"

"Why not? The professor found the Blathnait necklace, and it's in Ireland." Emma pointed to the photo credit under the picture of the Blathnait necklace. " 'Photo courtesy of the National Museum of Ireland,' " she read aloud. She turned to the professor. "If you were me, where would you look next?"

The professor grinned his leprechaun's grin. "She has a point, Tyler. You must admit, she has a point."

"But this thing could be worth a fortune. I don't like the thought of you traveling with it alone." Sam frowned. "I promised my father I'd work at his law office this summer."

"The law, Tyler?" The professor regarded Sam with amusement.

"It's my penance for studying computer art. My father thinks a summer with the law will change my mind."

Emma's mind raced ahead, to Ireland. "The Emerald Isle," she said.

"Emma—"

"Sam, this is something I have to do." She tucked the owl torque in a pocket of her photographer's vest and zipped it shut. "Thank you, Professor, for everything." She gave him a quick hug. "Let's go, Sam. I've got travel plans to make."

"Can't you talk any sense into her?"

"Sam is right, too," the professor said. "If your owl proves to be an authentic Celtic antiquity, it will be quite valuable—even without the other half. Should you find the other half... " He shook his head. "There would be no estimating its value. You must be discreet and careful."

"Don't worry. I will be very careful, I promise." Emma grinned at him and headed out the door, wondering how long it took to fly from Chicago to Dublin.

CHAPTER EIGHT

On the way home on the commuter train Emma could think of nothing but Ireland. She would talk of nothing else—despite Sam's worry about her traveling abroad alone.

"I can use my inheritance to finance the trip," she told Sam.

"What about college? That's your education fund. You know how expensive Brooks is."

"I can work my way through college, Sam. And I don't have to go to Brooks. Besides, I can always sell the house if I have to."

"You said you'd never sell your mother's house."

"I know, but ... " Emma's voice trailed off. She didn't want to sell her mother's house. It was all she had left of her life as a Lambourne, her only tie to life as she had known it until just a few weeks before.

Still, she had to find out who she really was. It was no good being a Lambourne if the rest of the family didn't recognize her as one. It hurt too much to be a Lambourne now. If she could find out where she came from, who she really was, maybe that would help the pain go away.

Ireland was the key to that all-important self-knowledge. She had to go. She turned to Sam with sad eyes. "The old gypsy woman was right, Sam. She told me I was descended from the kings and queens of ancient Ireland. And the Celtic owl torque is from Ireland, maybe even ancient Ireland." She grasped Sam by the shoulders, wanting him to understand why she had to go and why she couldn't wait for him to go with her. "Please try to understand. I have to follow this wherever it leads. Once I do, then I can come back. I'll know who I am and I'll be able to start my life over again."

Sam hugged her to him and whispered in her ear, "I'm scared for you. You're so obsessed with this thing. ... What if you get there and you don't find out anything? Then what?"

"I'll worry about that when it happens. *If* it happens." Emma wrapped her arms around him. She would miss him so much. She didn't know how she would have survived the past few weeks without him. "If the worst happens and I come back no wiser than before, you'll help me, right?"

"I'm not going anywhere, Emma." Sam stroked her hair. "I'll be right here waiting for you."

"Promise?"

"Promise."

They spent the remainder of the train ride home sitting there together, Emma's head on Sam's shoulder, Sam holding her tight. Neither said a word; they knew that she'd be gone soon and they'd be apart. As excited as she was at the prospect of her pilgrimage to Ireland, Emma hated the thought of leaving him. Torn between her growing love for Sam and her desperate need to find out who she was, Emma had to choose her search for herself.

But it seemed a terrible choice to have to make.

Emma opened the door to her house and screamed.

"Oh, my God," Sam said, looking into the hall from over Emma's shoulder.

The long entry was littered with shards of glass, splinters of gold-painted frames, and shreds of photographic prints. One such shred revealed her mother's sweet face, ripped above the brows. The same sweet face that Emma had not been able to look at after the funeral, the same sweet face she'd turned to the wall so she wouldn't have to look at it.

Emma lifted her head, away from the shattered images of her life, and looked past the entry into the living room beyond.

Involuntarily she shrank back. The living room, too, had been ravaged. Stuffing from her mother's beige couches blanketed the carpet, along with pages from art books and unearthed plants and pieces of broken knickknacks.

"Don't look." Sam held her tightly, then reached out and pulled the front door shut. "Let's get out of here."

"But Sam—"

"For all we know whoever did this might still be in there, Emma."

Sam had a point, Emma thought. "What are we going to do?"

"We'll go to my house," Sam said, taking her hand and running for his truck. "We can call the police from there."

Emma climbed into the truck and stared out the window at the place she'd called home all her life. Someone, for some unknown reason, had chosen to desecrate that home. She felt violated, unclean, unsafe. Sam pulled away from the house and sped down the street. Emma continued to watch her house until it disappeared in the distance. Only then did she allow the tears to come.

At Sam's house everyone was very solicitous about Emma. His mother, a petite woman with a big smile and a bigger heart, made her herb tea. His little sister, Amy, brought her an afghan; his little brother, Ben, contributed a handful of sticky M&Ms. Feeling numb, Emma curled up on a Victorian loveseat in Mrs. Tyler's parlor and let the friendly Tylers pamper her.

Sam called the police and arranged to meet them at Emma's house.

"I'm coming with you." Emma cast the afghan aside and scrambled to her feet.

"Oh, no you don't," chorused the Tyler family.

Emma smiled in spite of herself. "I appreciate your concern, but I'm fine, really." She turned to Sam, the most reasonable of the bunch. "I need to be there. I'm the only one who can tell what's missing."

"Sam will look for you," Mrs. Tyler said. "You can look later, when you're stronger."

"Sam, I *need* to go." Emma appealed to him for help.

"Emma can handle it," Sam said. He regarded his mother solemnly. "She's survived worse than this."

"Poor child," said Mrs. Tyler. "At least have another cup of tea first."

"Later, Mom," promised Sam. "Officer Jameson is waiting for us." Before his mother could say anything else, Sam ushered Emma out the door.

When they pulled up in front of Emma's house the police were already there. Officer Jameson introduced himself and took their statements—which didn't take long, considering they didn't know much except that they had come home and found the place ransacked.

"Ready for a little tour?" asked Officer Jameson.

Emma braced herself for the worst. "Sure," she said with more confidence than she felt.

Slowly the officer led them through the house. Room by room, they surveyed the damage. It was savage and complete—nothing had been left untouched. In the living room, Emma shuddered at the sight of her mother's beloved Queen Anne desk thrown to the floor, the drawers ripped out, writing paper scattered everywhere.

Her mother's Victorian cut glass collection lay shattered in the dining room, each shard catching the light and casting odd rainbows around the devastated room.

Nobody said anything. There wasn't much to say. Emma held Sam's hand tightly. They followed Officer

Jameson upstairs, where they inspected the bathrooms and guest bedrooms. The destruction was just as bad up there as it had been downstairs. Still, Emma was not prepared for the terrible spectacle that awaited her in her mother's bedroom, that beautiful oasis of cream-colored satin and white lace.

There was nothing ladylike about the room now. The elegant four-poster bed had been stripped down to the mattress, which was now pocked with slash marks and protruding springs. Emma reached down and picked up a sliver of cream-colored silk. Her unbelieving eyes filled with tears.

"You really shouldn't touch anything, miss," Officer Jameson said, his voice soft.

"Sorry," Emma whispered. She let the smooth silken tatter slip from her fingers. It fell silently to the plush white carpet, now strewn with the litter of her mother's life.

They saved Emma's own bedroom for last. Staring down at the mangled remnants of her childhood—souvenirs, posters, scrapbooks, dolls, stuffed animals, trinkets—Emma suddenly felt very old. The child who had grown up in that room had been destroyed as surely as those childhood things.

The final blow came as they inspected Emma's darkroom. Seeing her work so systematically ravaged proved one shock too many. Without a word Emma ran out of the darkroom, through her bedroom, down the stairs, and out the door. She could feel her chest folding in on itself; she couldn't breathe. She needed air. She gasped, gulping in the warm May air.

She heard the door slam behind her.

"Emma, are you all right?" Sam's voice seemed very far away.

"She needs to sit down," Officer Jameson said, gently helping Emma ease herself into a sitting position on the steps. "Breathe deeply," ordered the policeman.

Emma did as she was told. Calmer, she faced the officer. "As far as I can tell, nothing is missing."

"Seems strange," the officer said. "After all, there were a lot of valuables left behind—like your mother's jewelry. Most of the break-ins we get in this neighborhood are done by thieves who are after valuables they can sell easily to get cash for drugs."

"There's something so *mean* about it," Emma said. "If they didn't find what they were looking for, why didn't they just leave? Why destroy everything?"

"Nasty business," agreed the officer. "Do you have any idea what they were after?"

"No," Emma lied. She didn't want to tell this nice policeman about the owl torque; she didn't want another nice man telling her not to go to Ireland alone. She looked at Sam hard, willing him not to contradict her. "I'm so tired." She stood up quickly before Sam could say anything. "Do you think Sam could take me home now?"

"She means to my house," Sam explained. "She'll be safe there."

Officer Jameson did not seem convinced. "See that she stays there—at least until I see what the lab comes up with."

"I'll stick to her like glue," Sam promised.

That's what you think, Emma thought, more determined than ever to find out the truth about herself. First they'd taken her mother away from her, and now they'd taken her memories, too. Her childhood was lost to her forever—buried in the rubble of the place she had once called home.

Emma had to find a new home, and the search for that home would begin on Irish soil.

"I want to come with you," said Sam. They were sitting outside on the swing on the front porch of Sally's house, where Emma had been staying since the break-in. It was nearly dark now, and one by one the stars appeared in the early summer sky.

"You can't come with me," Emma said. "You promised your father you'd do the internship."

"I know," he admitted. "But there's no way I can let you go over there alone—not after what happened. It's too dangerous."

"Sam—"

"Whoever broke into your house is still out there, Emma. And from what Professor Herman says, they're not likely to go away until they get what they want."

The good professor had called Sam a couple of days after the break-in. He'd done some further research on ancient Celtic torques.

"Ancient Celtic jewelry is very popular on the black market," Professor Herman had told Sam. "And torques draw the handsomest prices." According to the professor, a prized torque had disappeared from a private collectors home in Chicago not long before. The police had come no closer to finding the thief than they had to finding whoever had trashed Emma's house.

"So, I'm going with you," Sam repeated.

Emma snuggled up against Sam, secretly relieved. She would never have asked him to go with her, but he *was* volunteering. Since the break-in, she'd suffered nightmares, awful epics in which she searched the labyrinthine streets of Dublin for the other half of the owl torque, only to find herself drowning in the rubble of her own home.

As much as she hated to admit it, the thought of charging off to a foreign country halfway around the world by herself intimidated her. Oh, she'd do it, Sam or no Sam—but how much less scary and more fun it would be with Sam. Still, she knew his father wouldn't like it. "What will your father say?"

Sam grinned at her. "I've already talked to him about it. He wasn't crazy about the idea, but I finally convinced him to let me go."

"And the internship?"

"I promised him I'd make it up to him next summer." Sam kissed her lightly on the lips. "That gives me another whole year to get out of it."

Emma laughed and kissed him back. "Ireland, here we come!"

"I wish I were going with you," Sally said as she waved good-bye to Emma and Sam at the airport gate.

"No, you don't. You've been planning your senior summer all year. You're booked through August." Emma gave her a quick hug.

"September." Sally wiped away a stray tear.

"Besides, you're in enough trouble with your parents for bringing me home. You need the rest of the summer to make it up to them."

"No way." Sally hugged Emma again. "Now you be careful." She hugged Sam. "You too."

"Last call for flight seventeen-oh-three to Shannon."

"That's us," said Sam. "We've got to go."

"I'm going to miss you so much." Emma smiled through her tears at her dearest friend. "I promise to write every day."

"You'd better," Sally said. "Sam, take good care of her. Now get out of here, before I totally ruin my makeup."

The hard rain did not keep flight 1703—nonstop from Chicago's O'Hare International Airport to Shannon International Airport—from taking off on schedule. From her seat in the plane Emma stared out of the small window at the gray, wet city she'd lived in all her life.

She was excited and scared and happy, all at the same time. As the plane taxied away from the terminal Emma looked away from the window, regarding the books in her lap with anticipation: *Birnbaum's Ireland,* the *Insight Guides* book on Dublin, *Women of the Celts, The Magick of the Tarot.* She'd spent the past two weeks reading everything she could about Ireland, her history, and her people. She'd also been boning up on the ancient Celts. She wanted to ready herself for her journey as thoroughly as possible; now that it was upon her, she felt ridiculously unprepared. Sally had suggested that Emma go back to Madame Rose for another reading, to get an idea of what to expect on the trip. But the last tarot reading had preceded such trauma that she didn't have the courage to do it. If anything terrible was going to happen, Emma didn't want to know about it.

"What are you thinking about?" Sam asked her as the plane began its race down the runway.

Emma turned to Sam with a smile. "Off we go," she said as the plane left the ground. "Ready or not."

"You're as ready as you'll ever be, Emma. I'm just along for the ride." Sam squeezed her hand. "You've done everything you possibly could, you know. You're practically a walking Irish encyclopedia. Don't worry, you'll find out who you are."

Emma kissed him on the cheek, then turned back toward the window. The plane climbed high above the city; Emma watched as her beloved Windy City disappeared from sight.

"Good-bye, Chicago," she whispered. "Good-bye, Emma Lambourne."

CHAPTER NINE

Somewhere over the Atlantic Ocean, Sam dozed off. Emma was much too excited to sleep, so she had turned over her window seat to Sam and settled into his on the aisle. She didn't want to have to crawl over him should wanderlust strike. Across the aisle sat a sweet-looking elderly woman knitting a red wool scarf. Emma exchanged polite smiles with the woman, then opened *Birnbaum's Ireland* and went over her itinerary one more time.

She and Sam would land at Shannon International Airport in Shannon, then make the short commuter flight to Dublin. In Dublin they would rent a car and drive into the Old City. There, Emma had made arrangements for them to stay at a small guesthouse called Danu House. Emma knew the ancient Irish kings and queens, the Tuatha De Danann, had worshiped the goddess Danu. She felt this was a good omen; that, coupled with the reasonable room rates, had prompted her to choose Danu House. Its central location was also a plus; the guesthouse was within walking distance of many of the places Emma and Sam would explore first. Their first stop would be the National Museum of Ireland, known for its unparalleled collection of ancient gold objects—including the Blathnait necklace they had seen in Professor Herman's book.

Involuntarily Emma placed her hand over her heart, feeling for the owl gold piece that lay hidden in an inside chest pocket of her photographer's vest. With it were several pairs of Emma's own earrings and a couple of bracelets to serve as camouflage should the customs officials who would be waiting for them once they landed in Ireland take any special interest in it. She wanted them to think the owl gold piece was just another piece of jewelry.

"Is this your first trip to Ireland?"

The cultivated European voice startled Emma. She looked up across the aisle. The little old lady and her knitting were gone. In her place was a thin, elegant man with dark eyes and thick salt-and-pepper hair. He seemed very Continental, very sophisticated, very much like the hero in one of those witty black-and-white films from the forties her mother had loved to watch on the American Movie Classics channel.

Emma smiled at the distinguished gentleman. "This is my first trip *anywhere.*"

"You are from Chicago." It was a statement, not a question.

"Born and raised." Emma extended her hand across the aisle. "Emma Lambourne."

To her surprise, he lifted her hand to his lips. "I'm very happy to meet you, Miss Lambourne. My name is

Vincent Archer." He squeezed her fingers slightly before gently releasing her hand.

No one had ever kissed her hand before; Emma found it thrilling somehow. "Call me Emma," she told him. "Are you from Ireland?"

"It's a beautiful country," he answered cryptically. "I visit as often as I can." He pointed to the book in her lap. "The Celts were a fascinating people. I particularly enjoy the stories of their great hero Cu Chulainn."

Emma nodded. She'd read about this Celtic hero; he was sort of the Paul Bunyan of ancient Ireland. She regarded Mr. Archer shyly. "I'd love to hear one of those stories—if you'd like to tell one."

The handsome man beamed. "I should be honored." He thought for a moment. "Since you are such a lovely young lady, I shall tell you the story of another lovely young lady." He leaned across the aisle. "I shall begin in the traditional Irish way." He cleared his throat. *"Fadofado,"* he began, "or a long, long time ago. If I were there then, I wouldn't be there now; if I were there now and at that time, I would have a new story or an old story, or—" He stopped and grinned at Emma. "Or I might have no story at all."

Emma laughed. "This is great," she said. "Go on, please."

"This is the myth known as 'The Rebellion of the Flower Daughter,'" he said. "It's the story of Blathnait, the most beautiful and perfect maiden in the world. The name *Blathnait* means 'flower.' You see, she was not born, but rather created out of flowers by the heavenly gods for the great hero Cu Chulainn. She loves him with all of her flowered heart. And he loves her."

Blathnait. Emma couldn't believe it. The very first foreigner she'd met was telling her the story of Blathnait—as in the Blathnait necklace. What synchronicity! Emma's heart leapt at the luck of it; with such luck she'd easily find out who she was.

"But the Dog King," continued Mr. Archer, "ruler of the hellish underworld, steals her away to be his wife, where he forces her to reign as queen of the underworld. She hates her husband, who has the face and temper of a rabid dog.

"Blathnait longs for Cu Chulainn, and he for her. Together they plot a plan for escape. Like Samson, the Dog King can be stripped of his strength. Blathnait tricks her husband into revealing the secret of his powers, and tells Cu Chulainn how they can weaken her cruel husband. Cu Chulainn performs the necessary tasks: he captures a salmon from the sacred spring, and finds the magic apple inside. He then presents Blathnait with the apple. Blathnait draws her unsuspecting husband a bath and ties his long hair to the bedposts and bedrail. Then she takes his sword and gives it to Cu Chulainn, who slices the apple in two."

"Does it work?" asked Emma, skeptical.

"The Dog King weakens at once, turns into an eagle, and flies away. Cu Chulainn and Blathnait reunite, and leave the underworld."

"And they lived happily ever after." Emma clapped, thinking the story was over.

"Not exactly," said Mr. Archer. "Remember, this is Ireland." He paused. "Safely home, Blathnait and Cu Chulainn spend many wonderful days together. But the Dog King's loyal court magician plots revenge. To spare her beloved Cu Chulainn's life, Blathnait runs away to the mountains beyond the Shannon River.

"The Dog King's court magician overtakes Blathnait there. He transforms the beautiful Daughter of the Flowers into an owl, the bird with the flower face. She becomes the Lady of the Night, the goddess of wisdom." Mr. Archer stared at Emma, his dark eyes shining. "Even now after dark you can spot her, all wise and all knowing, calling *'Cu cu cu!'* But her mournful call for her lover, Cu Chulainn, is forever unanswered."

"Poor Blathnait," said Emma, nearly moved to tears. "What a sad story."

"A little sad, yes," he agreed. "But very beautiful. Just like Ireland herself."

Emma thought about it. Mr. Archer was right. Throughout their long and turbulent history the Irish people had suffered invasion, oppression, and famine; even now the Troubles—as the Irish called the conflict in Northern Ireland between the Catholics and the Protestants—persisted.

The bitter with the sweet—that was Ireland. But Emma had already suffered the bitter back home; for her, Ireland would be only sweet.

She checked her watch. Four more hours. She could hardly wait.

Emma thanked Mr. Archer again, then excused herself to make her way to the restrooms at the back of the plane. Most everyone was asleep now, wrapped in thin Aer Lingus blankets, heads nestled against tiny Aer Lingus pillows. Emma's photographic mind recorded each dozing passenger, framing the faces as if for portraits.

She wished she knew their stories. Why were they going to visit the Emerald Isle? Business? Pleasure? Family? She wondered why Mr. Archer was going. She'd ask him when she got back to her seat.

But by that time he was gone. The little old lady was back in her place, asleep, her knitting needles idle in her lap. *How odd,* Emma thought as she slipped back into her seat. A sliver of fear pricked her spine; she wondered briefly who Mr. Archer was and what he wanted with her. She felt ashamed of herself almost immediately. Ever since the break-in, she'd been unusually suspicious of people. Jumpy, too. All the man had done was tell her a charming story. To assuage her guilt, she decided to try and find him once they landed, to say good-bye. With that chastening thought she closed her eyes, finally succumbing to the same traveler's fatigue that had snared Sam and the other passengers. She fell into the restless sleep common to air travelers, and dreamed of enigmatic strangers accosting her on dark, crooked Irish streets.

"Emma! Emma, wake up!" Emma felt Sam's warm breath on her neck. She opened her eyes to find his handsome face close to hers. He was whispering in her ear. "We're about to land, Emma. Wake up!"

She grinned at him. "We're there already?"

Sam grinned back. "Yep. Look out there."

Emma sat up in her seat and leaned past Sam so she could see out of the window. What she saw was an island of green dotted with clouds floating in the middle of a midnight-blue sea. "It's beautiful." She held her breath as the plane hurtled toward the thin ribbon of runway below, and she didn't let it out until the wheels hit the ground.

When she stood up to deplane she felt dizzy. Her body swayed and her head swam.

Sam caught her elbow to steady her. "Are you all right?"

"Yeah. Just excited, I guess." She retrieved her back-pack from under the seat.

"I'll take that for you." Sam slung Emma's backpack over one shoulder and his own over the other. Together they followed the rest of the passengers off the plane. Emma kept an eye out for Mr. Archer—she wanted to thank him again for telling her the story—but she never saw him. They proceeded to the international baggage claim area, where they collected their bags.

Customs was next. Emma stood with Sam in line, trying not to look as nervous as she felt. She was carrying what could be a national treasure of Ireland; she was so afraid that the customs officials would find the gold owl piece, recognize its possible value, and take it away from her. Willing herself not to reach for the hidden chest pocket of her vest, she watched the customs officials as they examined her fellow travelers' luggage. They did not open every suitcase; rather, they appeared to select one or two pieces at random and then rummage through them. They weren't as thorough as Emma imagined they might be. The knot in her stomach loosened somewhat.

Soon it was nearly their turn. Sam began to load their bags on the slow-moving conveyor belt as the customs officials inspected the businessman in front of them. He was a well-dressed Chicagoan in a three-piece suit and a heavy overcoat. They asked him to remove the overcoat; Emma tried not to panic as he handed it over.

What if they asked her to remove her photographer's vest? She looked at Sam, who smiled at her reassuringly.

"Isn't this great? I can't wait to get out of here and see some of the countryside," he said to her in his best all-American tourist voice.

"Me too," she answered. Sam was right; she needed to calm down and play tourist to get through this without causing any suspicion.

"Next, please," said the first customs official to Emma. She was a stout, stern-looking woman with a bullet-gray chignon.

"Hi," Emma said uncertainly.

"Please remove your vest," she said, passing Emma's suitcase to her male partner.

Emma stood there, immobile. Sam nudged her gently.

"Uh, sure." Emma slowly started to take off her vest, praying for a miracle. None came. She handed the customs official the vest. The woman began to open the pockets, examining the film, lenses, and other photographic paraphernalia she found in them. Emma held her breath when she came to the inside pocket. The woman pulled out a handful of the jewelry Emma had packed in along with the torque. She held it in her open palm and picked through the gold earrings and silver bracelets till she came to the torque.

"What's this?" Her voice was sharp.

Before Emma could answer, the male customs official tapped the woman on the shoulder.

"Look at this," he said, pointing to Emma's unzipped suitcase, which sat in front of him.

"Jesus, Mary, and Joseph," the woman said. She stuffed the torque and the rest of the jewelry into the inside vest pocket and handed it back to Emma without a word.

"What happened here?" asked the male customs official, swiveling the open suitcase around so that Emma and Sam could see inside.

"Oh, my God!" Emma stared at the gooey tumble of clothing and toiletries before her. Someone had ruthlessly explored every inch of the bag—even emptying her bottles of shampoo and conditioner.

"Are all of your bags like this?" The man's voice was strident.

"How should we know?" Sam went on the offensive. "The last time we saw our stuff was in Chicago—and it was just fine. Where has this luggage *been*?"

Neither customs official answered him. Ignoring Emma and Sam, they called a couple of their associates over and proceeded to investigate all of the bags. Each had been ransacked in a similar manner.

Emma watched in silence, her mind a jumble of contradictory thoughts. *Who did this? Why? When? How?*

"What's going on?" asked the passenger behind them. People began crowding around the conveyor belt.

Sam coolly regarded the customs officials. "Isn't the airline responsible for the safety of our luggage? Or does that responsibility fall on you?"

Again, the customs officials chose to ignore Sam's inquiries. "Come this way, please," said the woman.

Emma, calmer now, realized that she still had the gold piece. All she had to do was hold on to it. Quickly she slipped on her vest and hoped no one would notice.

The woman ushered Sam and Emma into a small room. Her colleagues followed with the bags.

"What were they looking for?"

"Who?" asked Emma.

"Whoever did this."

"I can't imagine," said Emma. "We didn't bring anything anybody would really want."

"Check to see if anything is missing," the woman said. It was an order, not a request.

Emma and Sam dutifully went through their things. As they expected, everything was there. Of course, much of it was torn, stained, or broken. Emma blinked back tears.

"We'll need to write up a report," the woman said stiffly. "We'll give the airline a copy; they should reimburse you for any damage."

"Look, we're exhausted. We've just come halfway around the world to *this.*" Sam indicated the suitcases.

"Can't we just leave our names and where we'll be staying and get out of here?"

The woman looked at Emma, whose eyes were now wet with tears. Softening somewhat, she handed Sam a form. "Fill this out. We'll keep the bags for now, but we'll be in touch."

"Thank you," he said with genuine sincerity.

"Yes, thank you," Emma added.

Together they quickly completed the form and left.

"Welcome to Ireland," Sam said as soon as they had escaped from the terminal and hopped into the first cab they saw.

Emma burst into tears.

CHAPTER TEN

"Take us to your favorite pub," Sam directed the cabbie while Emma dried her tears and checked her camera. Rolled up in an extra pair of jeans and packed in her backpack, it had survived the trip without incident so far.

Emma just wanted to get away from the airport as fast as she could. She rolled down the window and leaned back in the seat, letting the cool Irish air wash over her. "We're out of here."

The cabbie drove them away from the airport in Shannon and out into the countryside toward the city of Limerick. Emma and Sam said little; they'd agreed not to discuss anything where strangers might overhear. They were supposed to be tourists, so they were going to act like tourists. They looked at the scenery.

It was beautiful country, low green hills ruffling greener plains. Emma nestled her camera in the crook of her arm and snapped away. Every now and then she'd spot old ruins in the distance, zoom in, and try to catch the picture on film. A couple of times she asked the cabbie to stop so she could get a closer shot.

"Emma, you can't shoot everything in your first thirty minutes in Ireland," Sam told her. "We'll never get there if we stop every time you see a picture."

"I know." Emma sighed. "It's just that everywhere I look, I see pictures—beautiful pictures."

"It is beautiful." He kissed her cheek. "So sit back, relax, and enjoy it. Enjoy the beauty."

"You sound just like Sally," Emma told him. She settled back into her seat next to Sam and tried to feel Ireland, not just frame it.

"What's that?" Sam pointed up the road to what appeared to be an ancient fortress.

" 'Tis where we're going, lad." The cabbie spoke with a thick Irish lilt that made Emma feel like dancing. "Bunratty Castle."

"Some pub," Sam said, impressed.

The cabbie laughed. "That's no pub, laddie. That's a proper castle—with a fancy collection of priceless paintings and furniture and art and such."

"I've read about Bunratty Castle," Emma said. "They still have medieval banquets in the great hall at night."

"Right you are, miss. There's a model village there, too, showing how the people used to live in the old days. The tourists like the place."

"What about you?" Emma grinned, knowing that with her camera she looked like the perfect tourist.

"I prefer the pub next door." The cabbie pulled up in front of a handsome old building. "Durty Nelly's."

Emma laughed and jumped out of the cab, pulling out her camera again.

"Emma—" Sam started.

"I've got to get this one." She snapped a couple of shots. "This is Durty Nelly's—probably the most famous pub in all of Ireland."

Sam stared at the rustic seventeenth-century structure. "I guess this means you earned your tip," he said to the cabbie as he paid him.

"You said to take you to my favorite pub. This is everybody's favorite pub." The congenial Irishman smiled. "If you're hungry, try the oysters."

Once inside the packed institution, they could see why everybody loved Durty Nelly's. It was like stepping into another world. Mounted elk heads and old lanterns lined the walls, sawdust covered the floor, and glowing fires crackled in open turf fireplaces.

Emma resisted the temptation to snap a couple of shots. She and Sam found a small table in the back by a fire. They looked around the room at the people, who appeared to be an equal mix of locals and tourists. Back home Emma was usually the only redhead in the room, but not at Durty Nelly's—redheads were everywhere in Ireland. Emma felt at home for the first time, despite what had happened at the airport.

"I think we can talk here," Sam said, checking over his shoulder. "It's noisy and nobody's paying any attention to us."

"I'm scared," Emma said.

Sam reached across the table and took her hand in his. "That's a sensible reaction, Emma. Whoever broke into our bags was looking for the owl. We're going to have to be very careful."

"Do you think it was Martin?"

"Maybe. Or maybe somebody working on Martin's behalf."

"I'm not crazy about getting on another airplane," Emma said. The original plan had been to fly on to Dublin on a connecting flight.

"Me neither." Sam glanced at his watch. "Besides, it's taking off about now."

"I'm glad we missed it. Why don't we rent a car here and drive to Dublin? It's only a couple of hours away."

"Are you sure you're up to it? You didn't sleep as much as I did on the plane."

"All I need is some of those oysters the cab driver told us about." Emma squeezed Sam's hand. "Thank God you came with me. If you hadn't been here, I might have just turned around and taken the next plane home to Chicago."

"No, you wouldn't have," Sam said. "You're the bravest person I know."

Emma flushed and changed the subject. "I'm so excited to be here at last." She again regarded the many red-haired Irish people in the room with interest. "Somebody right in this pub could be related to me."

Sam grinned. "It's true. For a guy who likes redheads, Ireland is heaven."

"Very funny," Emma said, punching him playfully in the arm. "Very funny."

After a delicious late lunch of fried oysters and chips, Sam and Emma took another cab to the Limerick Avis office and rented a car there.

"I can't believe we came all the way to Ireland to drive a Ford," said Sam as they got into the small Escort.

"I can't believe we're going to drive it on the wrong side of the road." Emma regarded the narrow streets of Limerick with trepidation.

"I can handle it," said Sam with confidence as he pulled into the early evening traffic. "You just take a nap, and I'll have you in Dublin before you wake up."

"Not a chance." Emma laughed. "As long as you have my life in your hands, I'm staying wide awake."

Emma didn't sleep a wink on the way to Dublin. Determined to put the incident at the airport behind her—for Sam's sake as well as her own—she spent the drive capturing more of the glorious Irish countryside on film.

Three hours and six rolls of film later, Sam and Emma arrived at Danu House in Dublin. The historic Victorian guesthouse looked like a country home plopped right in the middle of the city. An oasis for two tired American travelers from Chicago.

"It's perfect," Emma told Sam as they climbed up the front steps. "Just perfect."

The proprietress, Dana Kelly, met them at the door. She was a short, stout older woman with the face of an aging Irish angel. She wore the country tweeds most of the women her age there wore; they were oddly complemented by lots of exotic, heavy gold jewelry.

"Welcome to Ireland," she said in a husky voice, "and welcome to Danu House."

Emma introduced Sam and herself. "We're so happy to be here, Mrs. Kelly."

"And happy we are to have you, dear." The older woman looked down at their feet. "Your luggage in the car?"

"We don't have any," Sam explained. Mrs. Kelly looked at him inquiringly.

"It's a long story," Emma began. "Something happened at customs. ... " Her voice trailed off.

"Do come in and tell me all about it over a cuppa."

Sam and Emma looked at each other.

"A cup of tea," Mrs. Kelly said in answer to their blank faces.

"Sure." Emma smiled, first at Mrs. Kelly and then at Sam, as the friendly proprietress ushered them into Danu House.

"Let me show you the lay of the land here." Mrs. Kelly gave them a quick tour of the small guesthouse. Downstairs was a formal dining room, kitchen, parlor, and Mrs. Kelly's bedroom. Decorated in what could be described only as New Age Victorian, the delightful rooms featured the finest Irish lace curtains, overstuffed chintz sofas and chairs, and a plethora of crystals and zodiac and Celtic symbols.

"You aren't a Druidess, are you?" asked Emma with a grin, pointing to the pagan images. "The Druids were the mystic priests and prophets of the ancient Celts," she informed Sam.

"Oh, now, dear." Mrs. Kelly smiled. "I'm a good Catholic woman, as I should be." She paused dramatically. "But the good Lord has blessed me with the power to see things." She didn't explain further.

Emma nodded, stealing a glance at Sam. He winked at her.

"Your rooms are at the top of the stairs," Mrs. Kelly told them. "Go on and freshen up while I put on the teakettle."

Emma and Sam climbed the steep stairs to the second floor, Emma studying the pictures that lined the staircase wall. These simply framed posters bore the colorful faces of famous Celtic goddesses.

There was Morrigan, the red-haired goddess of battle and procreation, draped in a purple toga and carrying a spear in one hand and a raven in the other. Next was Brigit, the goddess of fire, inspiration, and healing, an elegant, serene queen enveloped in a flame-shaped halo of light. And finally Blathnait, the Flower Daughter, a golden-haired maiden dressed in a rainbow of petals.

"It's her." Emma stared at the slim, sad-eyed beauty before her. "Blathnait."

Sam stopped on the stair behind her. "She's beautiful, but she seems so unhappy."

"Yes." Emma pointed to the snow-white owl that spread its feathered wings at the feet of the Flower

Daughter. "That's what Mr. Archer said. That her story is sad and beautiful, just like Ireland herself."

"I wish I'd met your Mr. Archer," Sam said as they continued up the stairs. "He may be the one who trashed our luggage."

"I know. I've been thinking the same thing." Emma shook her head. "He seemed so civilized, so cultured. It's hard to believe he would do such a thing."

"What did he look like?"

"Tall, slender, dark," Emma said. "Very distinguished-looking."

Sam looked at her thoughtfully. "Sounds like the guy in Martin's store."

"The customer?"

"The customer." Sam frowned. "If he *was* a customer."

"He could be in this with Martin."

"Maybe."

They stood at the top of the landing. On each side were three bedrooms, each with its own bath. Their rooms were the first off the landing, on opposite sides of the hall.

"You take the pink room," Sam said, changing the subject, "and I'll take the blue room."

"I'm sure that's what Mrs. Kelly had in mind." Emma stepped inside what would be her home for the next couple of weeks.

CHAPTER ELEVEN

Decorated in an explosion of rose chintz, the room smelled of rose water and fresh linens. The four-poster mahogany bed was plump with European down pillows. Emma dropped her backpack to the floor and sank onto the bed.

Heaven, she thought as she stretched out on the soft spread.

"Emma?" Sam poked his head into her room.

"Come on in." Emma didn't want to move.

Sam plopped onto the bed next to her. "What do you think?"

"I think it's lovely. And I think Mrs. Kelly's lovely."

"I think *you're* lovely." Sam pulled Emma to him and kissed her.

"What would Mrs. Kelly think?" Emma managed to say after a few minutes.

"Maybe she already knows. After all, she can *see* things." A bell tinkled in the background, and Sam grinned ruefully. "Told you." He stood up and pulled Emma to her feet. "Just my luck—I finally get you alone in a foreign country and the concierge is a psychic."

Emma giggled. "I think it's teatime."

The bell sounded again, and they made their way downstairs to the parlor, where Mrs. Kelly had set out quite a spread. "You've arrived just in time for afternoon tea," she told them. A splendid Wedgwood teapot sat in the middle of the carved Victorian tea table, surrounded by cucumber sandwiches, tiny sausages, biscuits, blueberry scones, thick cream, and fresh strawberries.

"Wow," said Emma.

"Wow is right," added Sam.

"Sit down and relax a bit," Mrs. Kelly ordered. She poured tea for them while they helped themselves to the home-baked goodies before them.

"These scones are wonderful," Emma said.

"Unbelievable," Sam mumbled, his mouth full.

"Thank you." Mrs. Kelly beamed.

As Emma sipped her first warm cup of tea she felt the stress of the day flow out of her. Her tense, tired muscles melted, her agitated gray cells settled down. "I feel almost human again," Emma told Mrs. Kelly. "I can't thank you enough for going to all this trouble."

"No trouble at all. Now, finish up. You need to sleep off that jet lag and you'll do it better on a full stomach."

"I couldn't eat another bite, really," Emma said.

"Don't worry, Mrs. Kelly." Sam helped himself to another cucumber sandwich. "I'm a growing boy, you know."

"Of course you are." Mrs. Kelly patted Sam's hand. "Now, Emma, you tell me that long story about your luggage while our Sam here has his fill."

Emma looked at Sam.

"Go ahead," he said.

He was right, Emma decided. After this warmhearted welcome, Mrs. Kelly deserved the truth. At least, some of it.

Emma told the story as instructed, leaving out the part about the owl piece and why they'd really come to Ireland.

"How terrible for you," Mrs. Kelly said. "What you must think of Ireland and we Irish!"

"Oh, we don't blame Ireland or the Irish," Emma protested. "Crime is everywhere. Besides, you've shown us that the Irish deserve their reputation as one of the world's most hospitable peoples."

Mrs. Kelly patted Emma's arm. "Thank you, child."

Sam yawned. "Go on up to bed, Sam," Emma said. Sam said good night and went upstairs to bed. Emma got up, too. "Let me help you clean up, Mrs. Kelly."

"Nonsense. You are my guests, after all."

"I insist."

"You really should be in bed," Mrs. Kelly told her. "A good night's rest will help ease your jet lag."

"I'm too excited to sleep." Emma placed their plates on the tea tray, picked it up, and carried it into the kitchen.

Mrs. Kelly followed her with the rest of the plates, and together they did the washing up in Mrs. Kelly's quaint Irish kitchen.

Standing there at the sink in the cheerful blue-and-yellow room, drying the dishes as Mrs. Kelly washed them, Emma was immediately at home, almost as if she'd been there before. She realized with a start that she'd felt that way ever since she set foot in Danu House. She regarded Mrs. Kelly with curiosity. What was it about this woman and her home that made her feel so comfortable, so cozy, so safe?

Mrs. Kelly smiled at her; she smiled back.

"That's the last of it," Mrs. Kelly said, drying her hands on a linen towel. "Now off you go to bed."

Emma knew she should go to bed, but she was reluctant to leave the serene company of Mrs. Kelly. "What did you mean about seeing things?"

Mrs. Kelly did not answer at once. "You haven't told me everything about your trip, have you?"

Emma stared at the woman. "You really can see things?" she asked.

"I don't pry." Mrs. Kelly led Emma to the long mahogany table in the dining room. "You don't have to tell me anything," she said enigmatically. "Let me show you." She waved Emma onto a Queen Anne chair, then switched off the overhead lamp. Lighting the tall white candles in the silver candelabra that served as the centerpiece, Mrs. Kelly chanted in Gaelic.

"Shan Van Vocht," she intoned. "Mother Ireland, anger of fire, fire of speech, breath of knowledge, wisdom of wealth, sword of song, song of bitter edge," she said, sitting down across from Emma. From the seat next to her she picked up a beautiful crushed-velvet bag of the deepest blue, embroidered with shining golden moons, suns, and stars. She loosened its gold cord and gently removed a stack of cards. The cards were different from the cards Madame Rose had used: they were smaller and more otherworldly. The backs featured an intricate Celtic diamond design, an elegant jeweled mosaic of emerald greens, ruby reds, amethyst purples, and sapphire blues.

Still, there was no mistaking what they were—tarot cards. Emma bolted from her chair. "I'm sorry, Mrs. Kelly," she stammered, "but I can't—"

Suddenly overcome by fear, Emma could not speak. She stood rooted to the floor, unable to move.

Mrs. Kelly came around the side of the table. "My dear," she said, placing her hands on Emma's shoulders, "there's nothing to be afraid of."

"Yes, there is." Emma sank back into her seat, remembering the terrible truth of Madame Rose's predictions. *The world as you know it will be turned upside down.*

"You've had a bad experience with the tarot." Mrs. Kelly sighed. "It happens so often. People who don't understand the power of the cards misuse it."

"Madame Rose knew." Emma's voice shook. "She knew too much, too much."

Mrs. Kelly sat down again. She took Emma's hand and held it in her warm palm. "What did she know?"

The touch of Mrs. Kelly's hand soothed Emma. Almost against her will, Emma began to tell Mrs. Kelly everything, from her encounter with Madame Rose to the incident at the airport. She wasn't sure why she told her, but she felt compelled to; she trusted her completely.

Mrs. Kelly listened quietly, without interrupting. She gazed unblinkingly at Emma, nodding now and then, concentrating on Emma's story. When she finished, Mrs.

Kelly squeezed her hand again. "You've been through a good deal, young lady. And I expect you're going to go through a good deal more."

"I suspect you're right, and that's why I don't want to know what's going to happen," Emma said. "It hurts too much."

Mrs. Kelly patted her hand. "I can understand that, but you obviously have made some enemies, and sometimes the cards can help us deal with our enemies. Forewarned is fore-armed."

Emma thought about it. The wise Mrs. Kelly had a point. "Maybe you're right." She watched Mrs. Kelly spread the colorful cards before her. "These cards are different from the ones Madame Rose used."

Mrs. Kelly smiled. "This is the Celtic tarot. It incorporates the magic and wisdom of the Druids."

"So you are a Druidess."

"Not exactly. But I do believe that we should take wisdom wherever we find it. And the Druids were a very knowledgeable and powerful people. To become a Druid, you had to study for twenty years." Mrs. Kelly drew the cards together again, shuffled them, and then presented the neatly stacked deck in front of Emma. "Cut the deck into three stacks."

Emma studied Mrs. Kelly's face. Her white hair shone like a halo in the candlelight: she looked like one of those good dead saints the old Catholic women wore pictures of around their necks back home in Chicago. There was nothing to be afraid of, not from Mrs. Kelly.

Emma took a deep breath and reached for the deck. Her hand shook as she divided the tarot cards into three even piles, facedown. She stared at the three piles as if they held her fate locked in their elaborate Celtic maze. Perhaps they did.

"Turn the top card of the first stack over. The one to your left." Mrs. Kelly's husky voice reassured Emma.

"Here goes nothing," Emma said, flipping the card faceup.

"Number three, the Empress." Mrs. Kelly smiled. "The Celtic Empress is Queen Maeve of the Sidhe. The Sidhe are the faery people."

"Leprechauns," said Emma.

"Yes—the little people, we call them. They live underground in secret caverns." Mrs. Kelly pointed to the necklace Queen Maeve wore around her neck. This Celtic torque was the most elaborate Emma had seen so far—an intricate interlocking of gold, pearls, and carnelians.

"The Sidhe are famous for their artwork, especially their jewelry," Mrs. Kelly told her. "This is a torque, a Celtic necklace of pounded gold."

"What does all this have to do with me?" Emma panicked, wondering if Mrs. Kelly knew about the owl piece. Maybe Mrs. Kelly really was psychic.

"This is a very positive card," Mrs. Kelly said. "Queen Maeve and the Sidhe will help you achieve your desires, whatever they may be." She looked at Emma inquiringly.

Emma knew Mrs. Kelly suspected there was more to her story, but she wasn't ready to tell her—or anybody else—about the owl piece. It was too dangerous. She quickly turned over the top card of the middle stack. "The Knight of Swords," she read aloud.

The diversion worked.

"Oh, no." Mrs. Kelly regarded the scarlet card coolly. It pictured a knight holding a long scabbard and sitting on a mountain, while the black crows of death circled over his head.

"What does it mean?" The card looked ominous to Emma. Even as she asked, she wasn't sure she wanted to know.

"The Knight of Swords represents the enemy—a formidable foe. You seem so young to have made such an enemy."

Emma's hand began to shake. She flipped over the final card.

"Temperance," Mrs. Kelly said, her husky voice thick with relief.

This was a pretty card, Emma thought, with its bewinged and becloaked angel dipping her bare feet in a blue pool of water against a background of a golden setting sun. The angel held two pitchers in her pale hands and was pouring water from one to the other. A comforting image.

"Here in Ireland we have many sacred springs and healing wells. This is St. Brigid, patron saint of holy wells. She'll protect you from your enemies, and help you heal whatever wounds they inflict upon you." Mrs. Kelly smiled at Emma. "So you see, my child, it is true you face a stern struggle, but you have St. Brigid and the faery people on your side. As powerful as your enemies may be, St. Brigid and the faeries are more powerful."

"Faery people?" Emma realized with a start that Mrs. Kelly actually believed what she was saying. Faery people, secret enemies, holy wells: who could take any of that seriously? Emma grinned. She must be suffering from severe jet lag after all. "Thank you for the reading, Mrs. Kelly." She was a nice lady, but a little ditzy.

She stood up and said good night to her hostess. "It's been a long day."

"You go right on up, dear, and dream sweet dreams." Mrs. Kelly ushered Emma out of the dining room to the foot of the stairs. "And say a quick prayer to St. Brigid before you drop off to sleep. It couldn't hurt."

It couldn't hurt, Emma thought later as she snuggled under Mrs. Kelly's soft down comforter. The question was, would it help?

Emma reminded herself that she was in Ireland now. *When in Rome, do as the Romans do,* she chided herself. *So give Mrs. Kelly and her Druids the benefit of the doubt.*

"Protect me from my enemies, St. Brigid," Emma whispered, and promptly fell asleep.

Chapter Twelve

May 5, 1994

Dear Sally,

We made it—and believe me, it wasn't easy!

First, the good news. Ireland is even more beautiful than I imagined. It's more than just pretty scenery; the ancient landscape seems to speak to me, promising to reveal its secrets if I can just look and listen hard enough.

Oh, God, I sound like Mrs. Kelly, the proprietress here at Danu House. She's a real Irish character who claims she can "see things." But she runs a wonderful bed-and-breakfast—and serves a high tea you wouldn't believe. We love it here.

Now for the bad news. Someone broke into our luggage and totally trashed our stuff. They must have been looking for the gold owl piece. But, of course, they didn't find it. Sam thinks it may have been this man I met on the plane, but I can't believe that. He seemed too sophisticated, too cultured to be a common thief. Whoever the culprit was, we have to be careful, in case they're still following us.

We're off to the National Museum this morning, where, with any luck, we'll find out something about the gold owl torque—something that can help me find out who I am. The sooner the better, the way things are going.

Love,
Emma

P. S. You were right about traveling with a man—I don't know what I would have done without Sam.

P.P.S. I'm shooting lots of film so you'll see it all!

Twenty minutes after posting Sally's letter, Emma stood in the Treasury Gallery of the National Museum of Ireland, transfixed by the splendor before her. She had been to museums before—Chicago boasted a number of first-rate institutions—but she had never seen anything like this.

The gold relics gleamed in their glass cases—a breathtaking display of jeweled necklaces, brooches, bracelets, and earrings. The thought that her little gold owl piece might belong in such company in such a place thrilled and terrified her. Overwhelmed, she looked away from the riches displayed in the gallery and focused her photographer's eye on the building itself.

The Treasury Gallery was a magnificent setting for the Irish antiquities it housed. Several stories high, with a ceiling of glass upheld by ornate white wrought-iron trusses, the gallery itself, from its intricate patterned marble floor to its angel-carved columns, was a monument to Celtic art.

"I'm beginning to understand just how valuable your little owl might be," Sam whispered, forcing Emma's thoughts back to the reason for their visit.

"I know." Emma understood for the first time why whoever wanted her owl piece wanted it so badly. She fought the urge to feel for the owl still hidden in the chest pocket of the photographer's vest she wore.

"Let's take a closer look," Sam said.

Together they inspected each case, marveling at the bejeweled Tara brooch, the oak-and-bronze Cross of Cong, and the silver-and-bronze shrine of St. Patrick's Bell.

"Oh, my God," Emma said as they approached the next glass case. "There it is."

The Blathnait torque shone before them. "It's amazing," Sam said. "When you look at your half all you see is the owl. But here, with the two halves together ..." His voice trailed off.

Emma finished his sentence for him. "You see Blathnait's face, too. The flower face."

Sam put his arm around Emma protectively and looked over his shoulder at the visitors behind them. He leaned over and whispered in her ear, "Your owl torque looks just like this. It must be the real thing."

Emma realized Sam was right, and this realization struck her like a blow. "This is it," she whispered fiercely. "This is the key to my past."

She squeezed Sam's hand. "I have to talk to the curator now."

"You'll never get in to see him."

"Sure I will." Emma gave him a quick kiss. "Just watch me. But if I get into too much trouble—"

"I'll be right here."

Emma climbed the marble stairs to the mezzanine, where steel and silver relics in glass cases flanked the walls. Casually she inspected the relics, one eye on the museum guards, while Sam joined her on the second floor, positioning himself on the other side of the mezzanine. There were two guards downstairs; neither cast a glance upstairs. One lone guard walked the mezzanine. When he was on the opposite side, Emma began to inch toward the heavy mahogany door in the far corner of the mezzanine. A discreet brass sign on the door read *Museum Personnel Only.*

Emma carefully inspected the steel breastplate, worn by ancient Celtic warriors, that was in the case before her. On the other side of the mezzanine, Sam walked over to the guard and engaged him in conversation.

Thanks, Sam, Emma thought as she quickly pulled open the heavy door and slipped inside, into a long corridor. Closed doors lined the corridor; brass plates revealed the names and titles of the occupants.

Three doors down on the right Emma found the one she was looking for: *M. Maeve Collins, Celtic Antiquities Curator.*

Maeve, Emma thought happily. *Like Queen Maeve and the Sidhe. This is a good omen. Maybe Mrs. Kelly's tarot cards were right after all.* She took a deep breath and pushed open the door.

An auburn-haired woman sat at a wide mahogany desk working on a computer. At the sound of the door shutting behind Emma the woman said, "Come back later, Anna, I'm busy." She didn't bother to look up.

Emma retrieved a small notebook and pen from the left outside pocket of her photographer's vest. "Ms. Collins," she began, "I'm Emma Lambourne, from America, and—"

"I don't care who you are or where you're from," the woman said with irritation, still intent on her computer screen. "I'm busy and—"

"I've come all the way from Chicago to finish my thesis on the jewelry and craftwork of the ancient Irish Celts," Emma said in a rush. "I'm specializing in the torque, that tubular form of—"

"I know very well what a torque is, Miss ... " The woman looked up finally, seeing Emma for the first time. Despite her manner, she was very pretty, with eyes as green as Emma's, faintly freckled fair skin, and that beautiful auburn hair.

"Emma Lambourne." Emma stepped forward to shake the woman's hand. "I'm so happy to meet you, Ms. Collins."

The woman paled, staring at Emma as if she had seen a ghost. She did not offer her hand.

Emma wondered what she had done to provoke such a reaction. Nervous now, she chattered on. "I have such admiration for your work. The antiquities collection has really prospered under your direction and—"

"Who did you say you were?" Her voice was barely audible.

"Emma Lambourne, from Chicago."

"Emma Lambourne, from Chicago," echoed the woman. This time she shook Emma's hand. "Do sit down." Collecting herself, she waved Emma into a Queen Anne chair. "I seem to have forgotten my manners entirely. I do apologize. I was in the middle of a report. ..." She stopped and stared again at Emma. "What can I do for you?"

"I'm finishing my thesis on the jewelry and craftwork of the ancient Irish Celts," Emma repeated. Crossing her fingers, she lied, "With special emphasis on the torque."

"What university are you with?"

"The University of Chicago." Emma crossed her fingers again.

"Really?" Ms. Collins smiled. "A very good school. Which professors are you studying with?"

"Dr. Randolph Herman sent me here." That, at least, was the truth.

"I met him once at a conference. A lovely man." She smiled again, more genuinely this time. "And a gifted scholar."

Emma didn't know whether to laugh or cry—laugh because now Ms. Collins believed her, or cry because she might ask her more about him than she could tell.

"What exactly would you like to know?"

Emma would have to worry about it later. "I'm particularly interested in the Blathnait torque. I'm hoping you can tell me something about its discovery."

"The Blathnait torque." Her voice took on a very official tone. "The Blathnait torque was found during the excavation of the burial chambers at Knowth in the late sixties. There's a wealth of literature available about the Knowth excavation at the museum gift shop. And of course the National Library is to be recommended for further reading." Ms. Collins stood up for the first time, revealing a tall, slim figure. "And now, Ms. Lambourne, I must ask you to leave. I must get on with my work."

"I'd really like to discuss the excavation with you. Could I take you to lunch one day soon? Today, or tomorrow?"

"I'm afraid that would be out of the question." She indicated the door with a wave of her arm. "My days are very full," she said firmly, ushering Emma to the door.

Time to go graciously, Emma thought, before the woman physically threw her out. She'd have to research the excavation herself. Or find someone else to ask. Or try Ms. Collins again in a couple of days. She offered Ms. Collins her hand, saying, "It was an honor to meet you. Thank you for your time."

Ms. Collins's dark eyes softened for an instant, and she squeezed Emma's hand tenderly, rather than shaking it. "Good-bye, Emma. Good luck with your thesis."

Emma stepped out into the hall, then turned to say a last good-bye. But the curator had already shut the door behind her.

Chapter Thirteen

Ireland, 1975

Mary waited for Michael by the holy well, sitting on the old stone wall by the statue of the Virgin Mary, her bare legs hanging over the edge and splashing in the sacred water. Sometimes she felt as if she had spent her entire life waiting for Michael at the holy well. And after the next day, when he would be going away forever, she would probably still be there, waiting for the boy she loved to come back to her. Which he wouldn't do, because he was answering the call of God, and no Irish gypsy girl had ever won a tug-of-war with God. In all the stories that her mama had ever told about her people and their run-ins with God or the saints or the faery people, no gypsy had ever come out on top. Neither would she.

"Hello, Mary."

She jumped at the sound of his voice. She knew only too well what accompanied that voice—a tall, lean, handsome boy with dark, wavy hair and eyes the color of the sea at midnight.

"Don't be sneaking up on me that way, Michael Baird," she said as he sat down beside her. She punched him playfully on the arm, telling herself not to fall upon him madly and smother him with kisses, which was of course what she ached to do.

But she could not, not that day. It was Michael's last day with her. After years of being together, first playing together as children and later exploring a new kind of relationship as teens, Michael and Mary would part. Michael—her sweet poet—would become a priest. Mary had no idea what she would become. She had always believed that Michael would defy his family and his church to marry her, that their love was great enough to overcome the obstacles his mother and his God had placed between them. She had never planned a life without him, never even imagined one. As much as she loved him, she hated him, too—hated him for loving her and leaving her.

They'd spent many hours there in the well, swimming and kissing and kissing and swimming. They'd never taken the final plunge; Michael was too much the gentleman for that. He would never take advantage of her, even if she wanted him to. He was no gypsy, but the son of a rich man, a man of property and principle.

Michael caught her fist in his warm hand and held it fast. "I'm going to miss you, Mary."

Mary edged over to him. "You don't have to go, you know. You can stay here with me."

Michael drew her clenched hand to his lips and kissed her knuckles. "My mother wouldn't like that, would she? Nor would Father O'Grady and the brothers at the abbey."

"I need you more than they do." Mary slipped onto his lap, her wet legs dampening his trousers. "I need you more than God does."

"Don't say that," he gently chided her. "That's blasphemy."

"I don't care." Mary buried her face in Michael's white shirt.

"Now, Mary, don't cry." He pulled her chin up to his. "You are so beautiful." His dark blue eyes softened. "Why do you have to be so beautiful?" he asked her, his quiet voice revealing his pain. He leaned toward her, his lips brushing hers. Mary slipped off his lap as easily as she had slipped on.

"Obviously not beautiful enough."

"Mary, come back here."

Mary smiled at him ruefully. "You're off to a life of celibacy. You may as well start getting used to it."

Michael frowned. "Mary, it's God's will."

"How do you know what God wants?" Mary shook her head. "You're always thinking about what other people want—your mother, Father O'Grady, the brothers at the abbey, God. Don't you ever think about what *you* want?"

"I want what's right."

"And how can you be so sure what's right?"

"What God wants must be right."

Damn his piety, she thought. "How do you know what God wants?" she asked again. "You're not a priest yet."

"Even when I am a priest, I won't always know what God wants," Michael said quietly. "I must wait, as we all must, for a sign."

"You and Mama and your signs." Mary shook her head in disgust, sending her wild auburn locks flying. "You have your prayers and your priests and your visitations. Mama has her tarot cards and her faery people and her séances. Neither of you lives in the real world. But I, who live in the *real* world without God or the faery people to protect me, I have to take care of myself."

"And how will you do that?" he asked with concern.

"Here's how." Mary stood up and pulled a shiny gold bracelet from the pocket of her short, full skirt. "Remember the old jewelry we found behind that broken stone in the well?" She held it up to the light filtering through the trees overhead. The bracelet shone in the sun like a pot of gold. "I took it home and polished it up. Cleans up nice, huh?" She twisted the bracelet with her fingers. "And look at this." The bracelet came apart in her hands, forming two perfect curved pieces. "It's a puzzle." She twisted the two gold sections together again.

"Incredible," Michael said, taking the bracelet from her and examining it carefully. "I thought it was just a piece of junk, but now it looks like—"

"Like it's worth a fortune," Mary said with triumph. "Now, this is a *sign,* Michael. A sign that we should sell this and go off to America together."

Michael wasn't listening. "What craftsmanship. The way these two halves come together to make this owl face..." He gazed at the owl's emerald eyes. "It must be Blathnait."

"Tell me the story," she said to Michael. "You know how I love your stories." Michael was so smart—the smartest person she'd ever known. When she had met him at that very same holy well many years earlier, she could barely read. Michael had brought her books and taught her to read. Growing up, she'd spent little time in school; her family was always on the road in the winter, traveling from one town to the next, her mother scratching out a living as a fortune-teller while her stepfather drank away what little he made as a handyman. Each spring they settled down here on the edge of town for the shearing season, while her stepfather worked shearing wool.

Mary lay down on the damp stone wall, resting her head on Michael's lap. He placed the bracelet around her slender wrist, then stroked her hair and told her the sad story of the rebellion of the Flower Daughter.

Mary shut her eyes and let Michael's soft, deep voice transport her back to the Celtic otherworld. She identified with the beautiful Blathnait, and wept for her when the Dog King carried her off against her will. But by the time Michael brought the sad tale to an end, she was crying for herself as much as for the Flower Daughter.

"I'm going to end up just like her," she told Michael. "Sad and alone."

"That's not true." Michael held her in his arms. "Take that bracelet and sell it. Go to America and make a new life for yourself."

"I could never leave Ireland without you." Mary twisted the bracelet apart. She took one half and placed it in Michael's palm, curling his fingers around it. "Keep this, Michael, and think of me. If you ever change your mind, come back to me. I'll be waiting." She slipped the other half of the bracelet into her pocket, then scrambled to her feet. "Now go." She waved him away with a clenched fist. "Go, *now.*"

"But—"

"Don't argue with me." Mary pulled Michael up roughly by his shirtsleeves. She threw her arms around him and kissed him, kissed him as she imagined Blathnait had kissed her beloved Cu Chulainn.

Michael clung to her, responding with torn passion. She pushed him away. "Get out of here, Michael, before we do something we regret." She turned her back on him then, and waited for him to walk away. She sat there on the cool, damp stone of the holy well, unmoving, as his footsteps echoed in her heart. He was gone.

CHAPTER FOURTEEN

After Mrs. Kelly's enormous breakfast of porridge, lean Irish bacon, poached eggs, freshly baked bread with butter and marmalade, and many a cup of strong, sweet tea, Emma and Sam set off for County Meath in the Ford rental car. Home to many ancient Celtic ruins, County Meath was where the Blathnait necklace had been found, and Emma thought there was a good chance that it might be where she could find the missing half of her owl piece—and herself. Emma drove; Sam sat beside her, the picnic basket Mrs. Kelly had packed for them on the seat between them. "Just a bite for the road," she had told them, but after that huge breakfast, Emma knew better.

They headed northwest on the N2 road, out of Dublin into the rich, rolling farmland of County Meath. Sam, lulled by the rhythm of the wheels and a full stomach, promptly fell asleep. Emma didn't mind. *He looks so cute when he's asleep,* she thought. *Just like a little boy.*

She switched on the radio, and quickly found a station playing traditional Irish folk music. Many of the songs she knew from the time she had spent in the old Chicago Irish neighborhoods, where every pub featured a different Irish band.

She drove happily, enjoying the scenery and the music. The sweet strains of a lullaby filled the air.

Sweet babe, a golden cradle holds thee;
Soft, a snow-white fleece enfolds thee;
Fairest flowers are strewn before thee;
Sweet birds warble o'er thee.

Emma sang along with the chorus.

Shoheen sho lo,
Shoheen sho lo, lo.

She felt oddly at home in this foreign country, singing Irish songs and driving on the wrong side of the road, as if at some primeval level she knew she belonged there, in the home of her ancestors.

The road descended sharply as Emma approached the old stone bridge that crossed the river Boyne into the Valley of the High Kings. This was the land of ten thousand tales and a hundred thousand memories—an ancient place rich in legend, history, and prehistory.

On the far side of the bridge was the old village of Slane. Emma carefully maneuvered the small Ford down the steep road. *Whew!* she thought, looking over at Sam, who slept on, carefree and oblivious to his surroundings. How different this was from driving at home, Emma thought. Back in Illinois the land was flat and the roads were wide; in Ireland the land was hilly and the roads were narrow. And in quiet County Meath those roads seemed even trickier to navigate than they had in Dublin—despite the absence of traffic.

Emma crossed the one-lane stone bridge with a sigh of relief. She continued down the N2 road, which became the main street of Slane. The sleepy village was built right upon the steep bank of the river Boyne. Emma proceeded leisurely through the picturesque town, fighting the urge to stop and snap a few frames of film along the way.

She approached a crossroads where four matching gray stone Georgian houses stood at each corner like sentries. *What a picture,* thought Emma, her photographer's mind racing to identify the most attractive angle from which she should shoot the remarkable intersection. She reached for her backpack and fumbled for her camera, one eye on the road and the other on the bag.

She never saw the stop sign. But she did hear the horn that blared into her consciousness—just in time for her to slam on the brakes. The car jolted, screeching to a stop just inches from a brightly painted old VW van.

Sam was awake now. "What's going on?"

"Are you all right?"

"I'm fine." Sam looked around him. "Where are we?"

Emma didn't answer. The owner of the VW van had gotten out and was striding toward the Ford. Emma hurried out of the car to meet him. He was a handsome

Irishman, about her age, with blue eyes fringed with black lashes. Black curly hair peeked out from under his tweed cap. He didn't look too happy with Emma.

"I'm so sorry," she began. "I was looking at the beautiful buildings and—"

"What the hell are you doing?" he shouted at her. "Are you daft?"

"I'm sorry, but I never saw the stop sign."

Several townspeople had gathered round the intersection. The handsome young man played to the crowd.

"What were you doing, Miss America? Reading your guidebook?" The onlookers laughed.

Emma stiffened and felt her face flush. "If you must know, I was reaching for my camera. I'm a photographer."

"'I'm a photographer,'" he repeated in a broad midwestern American accent that parodied her own. "What were you going to do, Miss America, snap a photo of me as I met a terrible death at your hands?" He framed his face with his hands like a mime, then closed his eyes and let his head jerk to the side, as if he were dying.

The crowd laughed and applauded. Emma stood rooted to the spot, anger replacing remorse. How dare this stranger ridicule her like that, in public no less?

Sam obviously agreed with her. He slammed the door behind him as he got out of the car and headed for the insolent Irishman.

"Oooh," mocked the stranger in a fair John Wayne imitation. "Here comes the all-American hero to the rescue."

"I don't need rescuing." Emma had had enough. She stepped right up to him, positioning herself between him and Sam. "I can take care of myself," she said in a voice that confirmed the statement. "Look, I said I was sorry. No harm was done—you're fine and your van is fine. So why don't you just get back in it and get the hell out of my way?"

"You heard what the lady said," Sam said firmly. "Why don't you just run along now?"

"Why don't *you* just run along now?" echoed the stranger, moving forward so that Emma was sandwiched between the two young men.

"Stay out of it, Sam. I can handle this guy," Emma said, trying to hold her own.

"Yeah, Sam. From the looks of her, she can take both of us." He grinned at Emma. "Come on, Miss America, come and take me."

The men in the crowd whistled and whooped, egging their brash countryman on.

Out of the corner of her eye, Emma saw Sam pull back to throw a punch. She had to do something quickly, before these two idiots killed each other.

So she pulled the Irishman's cap down over his face. The crowd laughed.

Jerking the cap back on his head, he caught her wrist as she stepped away from him. The crowd fell silent; Emma could hear Sam breathing heavily behind her, ready to pounce.

To her surprise, the Irishman smiled. "I deserved that," he said cheerfully. He brought her hand to his lips and kissed it. "I apologize, Miss America." He released her hand, then proffered his own to Sam. "Devin O'Connor. Delighted to meet you. Sam, isn't it?"

Nonplussed, Sam nodded. "Sam Tyler."

Devin turned back to Emma, his blue eyes dark with humor. "And you are?"

Emma smiled in spite of herself. "Emma Lambourne."

"Emma," he said softly. "Emma of the emerald eyes."

Emma blushed. This guy was too much.

"We'd better be on our way," Sam said stiffly.

"Right," answered Devin, his eyes still on Emma. "I suppose you're off to see the relics."

Ignoring him, Sam headed back to the car. Emma knew she should follow him, but she wasn't ready to say good-bye to this Devin O'Connor quite yet. The crowd, sensing that the mini-drama was over, had dispersed. Emma and Devin were left alone in the intersection.

"Yes," she said. "We're on our way to Newgrange."

"You know, I'm sort of an expert on the subject," Devin said. "Newgrange is, of course, splendid, but there are many other sites of interest as well. Suppose I give you a tour?"

Emma regarded him skeptically. "Why should you do that?"

"To make up for my behavior earlier. Not too gentlemanly. I'm afraid I tend to get a little carried away. Let me make it up to you." He smiled at her, and suddenly she believed him.

"All right," she heard herself say.

"Just follow me. Oh, one more thing—let your friend drive," he said with a wink.

"Sure," she said. She laughed and headed back to the car.

Sam was going to kill her.

Sam drove along behind the VW van, muttering under his breath. Emma caught the occasional "clown" and "jerk" and "trouble," and smiled. That was one thing she loved about Sam: he would complain, but not for long. He was too good-natured to hold a grudge. She'd taken her camera out and was busy trying to capture all she saw on film. She never did get that shot of the Georgian houses in town. But she made up for it on the Hill of Slane, their first stop on the Devin O'Connor tour of the Boyne Valley.

"To the east, there," said Devin, pointing, "you can see the port of Drogheda, where the river Boyne meets the sea."

The three of them stood on the summit of the Hill of Slane, enjoying the remarkable view.

"To the south are the blue Wicklow Mountains, and to the west, the pastures of the central plain rolling away into the great bog of the Midlands," said Devin.

Emma snapped a few shots, then suddenly put her camera down. She stood there in silence, drinking in the beauty and the peace of the place. She was trying to do what Sally had advised her to do—experience Ireland, not just record it. As she stood there she felt an intense serenity calming her senses, lightening her spirit, and refreshing her hope.

Even if I don't find my biological parents in this strange and beautiful land, she thought, *I may still succeed in finding myself.* With a sigh, she turned back to Sam and Devin, who were discussing their next stop, the Brugh na Boinne—the Palace of the Boyne, burial place of the king and queen of the Stone Age pre-Celtic people.

"It's one of the most important prehistoric sites in Europe, dating from around 3000 B.C. The whole necropolis extends for several kilometers," Devin said. "See that low rise over that big curve in the river?" Devin pointed east again, toward Drogheda. "That's it."

This was what Emma had been waiting for. Newgrange, where the Blathnait necklace had been found, was one of the three great man-made earthen mounds there. Each mound contained burial chambers where the ancient pre-Celts had lain the ashes of their cremated dead. "Let's go," said Emma, slinging her camera over her shoulder by its thick strap.

Brugh na Boinne was only a few miles down the road from Slane. They could see the three great mounds—Knowth, Newgrange, and Dowth—from the road. They stood about a mile apart from each other, a trio of tumuli from the ancient past.

First they did what all good tourists traveling in that part of Ireland did—they toured Newgrange.

"Newgrange is the only one of the tumuli to be fully excavated and restored," said Devin as they approached the huge, circular mound of white and black borders covered with earth and grass, some 250 feet wide and nearly 40 feet high. "Knowth is under excavation now, so it's closed to the public."

"What about Dowth?" asked Emma, thinking of the Blathnait necklace.

"Dowth has been badly plundered," Devin said. "It's in pretty bad shape, although I'm sure we'll get around to excavating it sometime."

Emma grinned. "We?"

"The state of Ireland, I mean."

They followed a tour group into the Newgrange mound by way of an entrance overlooking the river Boyne. One by one they stepped into a long, narrow passage, which led into the interior of the mound.

There they found themselves in a central domed chamber some twenty feet high. Emma stared at the great stones around her, marked by carvings with the same intricate spiral and diamond patterns featured on the gold owl piece.

"Looks familiar, doesn't it?" whispered Sam in her ear.

"Yeah."

After a quick tour of the smaller chambers, they trooped back through the passage. Devin pointed out the small aperture over the outer entrance to the passage.

"That opening is precisely aligned so that the sun's rays will penetrate to illuminate the chamber only during the winter solstice."

"Why then?" asked Sam.

"To remind us that spring is coming. It's a symbol of rebirth and renewal."

Emma felt a tingling up and down her spine. "A symbol of rebirth and renewal," she repeated. That was what she was in Ireland for. She felt so close to the truth, there in the ancient holy place.

"Do you think we could walk over to the other mounds, just to check them out?" she asked Devin after they exited the mound.

"Sure. Of course, they won't let you in, but we can walk around."

So Sam, Emma, and Devin trekked up and down the Brugh na Boinne, Emma snapping pictures when something struck her as important. She was shooting by intuition now, not reason. They came across many other smaller remains; some had obviously been disturbed by plunderers and others were overgrown.

"Burial chambers are everywhere around here," Devin said. "All of the big rocks you see are called standing stones. They're a sort of ancient tombstone. Wherever you see one, there's a burial chamber."

"There's one thing I don't understand," Emma said. "We saw the Blathnait necklace at the National Museum in Dublin. They said it was found at Dowth, but it dates from around the first century. These mounds are thousands of years older."

"That's true," said Devin. "Nobody really knows how it got there, or why. Other treasures have been found in similar places.

"But we do know that these burial chambers have been looted by marauders, used as hiding places, even *lived* in by gypsies, among others.

"There's a famous Celtic legend that tells the story of Grianne, daughter of Cormac the Wise. The king promised her to an older man. On the night before her wedding she eloped with her young lover, Diarmuid. Pursued by the king's men, they hid in prehistoric tombs like these. That's why you'll often hear people call these standing stones 'the beds of Diarmuid and Grianne.' "

"What happened to them?" asked Sam.

"After years on the run, Diarmuid was killed by an enchanted boar, and Grianne was married as promised." Devin grinned. "Not a very happy ending, I'm afraid."

"They never are," said Emma.

"What do you mean?" Devin asked.

"Every Irish love story I've ever heard ends badly. Nobody ever lives happily ever after."

"That was a long, long time ago, Miss America." Devin touched her cheek. "Things are different now."

"It's getting late and I'm getting hungry, Emma," Sam said loudly. "Isn't it about time for that picnic lunch Mrs. Kelly fixed for us?"

"Well, I don't know." Emma looked around her. "I guess we've seen about everything. I've got a lot of pictures. What do you think, Devin? Have we missed anything? Do you think we should stop now?"

Devin regarded Sam with amusement. "Sure."

They walked back to the car in silence. Emma spent the whole time wondering when she would see Devin again and why she was so eager to see him and what was wrong with her, anyway.

At the car Sam turned to Devin and offered his hand. "Thanks for the tour."

Devin shook Sam's hand. "No problem," he said, putting on his American accent again.

Emma laughed. "Why don't you join us on our picnic? I'm sure Mrs. Kelly packed enough for an army. It will be our way of saying thank you."

"I'm sure Devin has better things to do than hang out with tourists like us," Sam said. "We don't want to impose."

"Nonsense. I've got all the time in the world." He clapped Sam on the shoulder as if they were old pals. "Besides, I know the perfect place for a picnic."

Twenty minutes later they were sitting on Mrs. Kelly's red plaid woolen blanket on the broad summit of the Hill of Tara. The 512-foot hill offered a magnificent view of a vast expanse of lush meadow.

Emma passed around the fine lunch Mrs. Kelly had packed for them: roast beef and Limerick ham sandwiches; smoked salmon and *boxty,* a kind of potato bread; soda bread, scones, and apple tarts; and two thermoses of hot tea.

"Thank you, Mrs. Kelly, wherever you are," said Devin as he bit into a sweet apple tart.

"Danu House," answered Emma. "That's where we're staying, at Danu House in Dublin. In the old city."

Sam glared at her. She knew he didn't approve of her telling anybody where they were staying, but she didn't care. Lunch would be over soon and Devin would walk out of their lives as easily as he had walked in. She didn't want that. There was something about him.... "Tell us about Tara," she said to Devin, hoping to prolong the luncheon as long as possible.

"Tara is a very special place," Devin said quietly, "in both Ireland's history and my own. You see, I am an O'Connor. That's the Anglicized version of *Ua Conchur,* which means 'grandson of Conchobar.' King Conchobar built Tara. It was a ringed fort, the cultural and religious headquarters of ancient Ireland for two thousand years."

"You are descended from the high kings of Tara." Emma stared at him, remembering the words of the old gypsy fortune-teller back home. "You're royalty."

Devin laughed. "Yes, me and the rest of the millions of O'Connors in the world." Devin spread his arms out as if embracing his heritage. "We Irish are in love with our ancient past. I'm proud to be an O'Connor—no matter how many of us there are. That's why this holy place is especially sacred to me."

Emma put down her sandwich and picked up her camera. "Go over there," she ordered Devin. "By the edge of the summit."

"Why?"

"I want a picture of the high king of Tara surveying his kingdom."

Devin dutifully scrambled to his feet and trotted over to the slope.

Sam frowned but said nothing as Emma jumped up, camera in hand.

She took her time figuring out how to frame the shot, using her feelings instead of her f-stops as her guide. Finally she found just the right composition. She focused in on Devin, standing tall on the Hill of Tara, the vast vista of western Ireland behind him, lit by the warm glow of the late afternoon sun.

She snapped the picture. It was perfect, and she knew she would keep it forever.

"Thanks for everything," Emma told Devin as she and Sam prepared to head back to Dublin.

"My pleasure." Devin opened the door for her as Sam slipped into the driver's seat. He pulled a card from his back pocket and handed it to Emma. "Here's my phone number at Trinity College in Dublin. Keep in touch."

Emma smiled, glad that he seemed as reluctant to say good-bye as she did. Could he possibly feel as inexplicably drawn to her as she did to him?

"You too. We're at—"

"Danu House." He finished her sentence for her. "I'm not likely to forget that."

"Good-bye, Devin," said Sam with an air of finality.

Devin grinned, shutting Emma's door and stepping back from the car. Sam pushed hard on the accelerator, and with a squeal of the tires they were off.

Emma leaned back in her seat and sighed in satisfaction. "Weren't we lucky to run into Devin?"

"I don't know."

"Come on, Sam, he showed us so much."

Sam didn't say anything.

"You don't like him, do you?"

"He's okay."

Emma regarded Sam with amusement. "If I didn't know you better, Sam, I'd say you were jealous."

"Please," Sam began, his voice thick with disgust. "Why should I be jealous of him?"

Emma laughed. "He is kind of a show-off," she admitted. "Still, it was a wonderful day."

"What was so wonderful about it? Sure, we saw some fabulous sights, but we didn't *learn* very much that can help you."

Sam was right. Emma bit her lip, thinking.

"Now that we've seen the place, I don't see how it can help us find out who you are. I don't even see how it could help pinpoint the other half of the owl piece," Sam continued. "Either somebody's already found it, or it's lost, or—"

"Or it's still out there somewhere."

"We can't dig up the whole Boyne Valley," Sam pointed out.

"No, we can't. And even if we could, it probably wouldn't help us find out who I am." Emma closed her eyes. *There has to be a way,* she thought.

"I don't mean to be discouraging." Sam reached over and touched her cheek. "I just think we have to go on to plan B."

"I know." Emma squeezed his hand. "You're right." She opened her eyes and sat back up in her seat. "I guess I had this romantic idea that I'd come to these fabulous ancient ruins and discover the truth about myself and the treasure. Pretty silly, huh?"

Sam smiled at her. "Not silly at all. And it may still happen."

"But in the meantime, on to plan B."

"We'll start tomorrow by going through all of the newspaper records in County Meath, since that's where the owl bracelet came from before they emigrated to America. Maybe that's where your parents came from."

"Great idea. Only I've thought of a source better than the local paper."

"What's that?" asked Sam.

Emma grinned. "The parish priest."

CHAPTER FIFTEEN

May 8, 1994

Dear Sally,

Just a quick postcard from Newgrange, where the ancient royal Celts are buried. We visited the burial mounds today and picnicked on the holy Hill of Tara with a true descendant of the high kings.

Ireland is a magical place—I feel at home here. I can't explain why I feel so connected to this foreign place, but I do. No matter what happens, the trip will have been worth it, just for today.

Gotta run—

Emma

The churchyard was deserted. Sam had dropped Emma off at St. Peter's on the outskirts of Navan, the county seat of Meath, on his way to the *Meath Chronicle.*

It was what the Irish called a soft day, veiled in a thin damp mist. Emma pulled the hood of her rain poncho up over her head. She wandered around the grounds of the high-Gothic church, but found no one.

The mist lent a spooky air to the place; Emma shivered in the damp. She sensed that someone was watching her, though she saw no one. She knocked on the front door of the rectory behind the church, but no one answered. Perhaps the parish priest—Francis O'Malley, according to the sign outside the church—was praying inside the church itself.

She pushed open the heavy carved oaken door and stepped into the dark, high-ceilinged church. It was more like a cave than a house of God, Emma thought, cold and forbidding. She'd read that St. Peter's had been built by a local saint, martyred at Tyborn in London in 1681. His head was preserved in a shrine right there in the church. Emma prayed she wouldn't come across it.

She walked slowly down the center aisle. Still she saw no one. Sam was across town at the *Meath Chronicle,* checking the weekly newspaper's records, looking for something—anything—that might lead them in the right direction. She had nothing else to do, so she decided to wait. Slipping into the front pew, she sat down and tried to talk to God. That's what her mother had always told her praying was: talking to God.

She hadn't been inside a church since her mother's funeral, and she certainly hadn't talked to God then—except to ask why. Why did her mother have to die? Why had her father died years before—before she had even had the chance to know him? And why this wild-goose chase halfway around the world to find her real parents, if they existed? And if they did, why should they want to see her? They had given her up, after all.

Emma sighed. Maybe she should just turn in the owl piece to that woman at the National Museum in Dublin and go home.

"Excuse me."

Emma felt a cold hand on her shoulder. She turned to find a tiny, heavily wrinkled old man staring at her. He looked like a little black bird in his dark priest's suit, the bright white collar at his neck. "Who are you?" he asked in a thin, wavering Irish lilt.

"Emma Lambourne," answered Emma with a smile, gently shaking his frail hand. "From Chicago."

"Don't know anyone from Chicago," he said flatly, peering at her closely with watery blue eyes. "Should I know you?"

"No," Emma reassured the old man. "We've never met."

The old man sighed. "Well, then, come along and we'll get the paperwork over with." He turned to go.

"What paperwork?" Emma was confused. Had she missed something? "What do you mean?"

Turning back, the old man shook his bald, freckled head. "Don't be daft. You can't get married without the paperwork."

"Married? *Me?*" Emma laughed. "I'm not getting married."

"Then what are you here for? Confession, communion, last rites?"

Emma shook her head.

"Ah," he said with emphasis, "I understand now. You wish to join the Church." He smiled for the first time, revealing his gums. "I do love a convert."

How to explain? Emma wondered. "I hate to disappoint you," she began, "but I'm not here for any of those reasons. I'm not here for religion."

The old man sighed, and lowered himself painfully into the pew next to Emma. "I don't understand. This is a church, my dear. Why come to a church if not for religion?"

Emma was not sure what to say to that.

The old man leaned toward her suddenly. "You're not an atheist, are you? I don't much like atheists in my church."

"Oh, no, I believe in God. Honest," Emma said quickly, keeping to herself the fact that she didn't know much about Him.

"Good." The old man regarded her with curiosity. "Then what do you want?"

Emma wasn't sure if she could make this funny, addled old priest understand. But she had to try. She took a deep breath and plunged in. "I'm looking for my parents."

"Are they lost?" The old man looked at her as if she were the addled one.

"I was adopted at birth, and raised in Chicago by Americans," Emma explained. "But I believe my mother and father were from here. Maybe you knew them."

The old man said nothing.

"I was born eighteen years ago, in the spring of 1976. Do you remember any young women from the parish leaving for America a little before that time? Maybe an unwed woman expecting a child?"

"I've been here fifty years," the old man said with pride. "During that time we have lost too many sons and daughters to America. I remember every child who emigrated from this parish." He looked away from her, staring off into the past. "I did not know your mother." The old man's thin voice was stern.

Emma found it hard to believe he could really remember back that far. "It was a long time ago," she said gently. "You may have forgotten. Perhaps if you think about it—"

"I did not know your mother," the old man repeated. "No young woman left County Meath at that time. I would have known." Abruptly he stood up, wincing as he did so. "I must get back to my duties now." Without another word he walked down the aisle and out of the church.

Emma stared after him, not knowing what to do. He was an old man; she didn't want to upset him. She sat there for several minutes, trying to figure out another approach. Finally she gave up, deciding to wait outside for Sam. Maybe she'd run into the old priest again, and another way to broach the subject would occur to her.

She left the church, her heavy footsteps echoing on the stone floor. Outside, the day's drizzle made the empty churchyard appear colder than ever. She walked to the road and peered up and down its length. No sign of Sam or the Ford.

It was a couple of miles into town. Emma decided to walk it, despite the dampness. She'd gone about half a mile when an old blue Rover rumbled past her. At the sight of the driver, Emma smiled. Another priest.

She turned around and strode purposefully back to the churchyard.

Fifteen minutes later, Emma sat in a big, overstuffed, faded chair in front of a blazing peat fire. "Make yourself at home," Father Michael said. He was a tall, distinguished-looking man, much younger than the old priest Emma had spoken to in the church. That was Father O'Malley, she'd found out, the senior parish priest. "I'll be right back with some tea."

Emma took off her wet poncho and settled back into the soft chair, warming her cold fingers near the comforting fire. Thanks to the chintz furniture and lace curtains, it was a cheerful room. Still, it was a room for men, lacking in ornament except for many books, a few religious statues, and the accouterments of a pipe smoker. The only personal note was a series of landscape photos that hung on the white walls—photos that, Emma guessed, revealed one of the priests' fascination with photography.

She got up and crossed the room to take a closer look. "These are very good," she told Father Michael when she heard him enter the room behind her. "Did you take them?"

"Yes, thank you." He set the tea tray down on a low serving table. "Just a rank amateur, of course, but I do enjoy it."

"I'm a photographer myself," Emma said, sitting down across from him as he poured steaming tea into two china cups. "You're more than just an amateur."

"Again, thank you." He handed her a cup. "That's a series I did depicting our local monuments and ruins."

"Yes, I know. We saw them yesterday. They were fantastic. I got some great shots." She leaned forward. "I recognize the Hill of Tara, and Newgrange. But where did you shoot that photo there on the far left?" Emma pointed to a striking black-and-white shot of an old stone watering hole.

"That's one of the many holy wells you'll find here in our county." He offered her a scone. "Here, try one. They're very good. Mrs. O'Bryan dropped them by for me just this morning."

Emma took one, just to be polite. She'd already had more than her fair share of Mrs. Kelly's scones that day. It seemed the Irish just couldn't get enough scones.

"What can I do for you, Emma? I don't know many Americans," Father Michael said.

Emma searched Father Michael's countenance for hints of his character. He had a nice face, the face of someone who had seen too much suffering but enjoyed life anyway. She would have liked to take his picture. "It's a long story," she began.

"We Irish love a long story," he said kindly, lighting a pipe.

So she told him everything from the beginning. He listened patiently, impassively, with a sort of serene concentration that Emma found both comforting and otherworldly.

"So what I need to know is," she said, wrapping it up, "do you know who my parents are? Do you know of any woman in your parish who left for America in 1975 or 1976? An unwed, pregnant woman?"

Father Michael sat very still, puffing on his pipe. The pungent smoke filled the air. Finally he said, "I was away at the seminary at that time. But Father O'Malley would remember. He—"

"I already asked Father O'Malley. He said no, but his memory might ... " Emma's voice trailed off.

"He's napping right now. But I might be able to persuade him to consult his records. He may have overlooked someone or something. I must warn you not to get your hopes up, however. This is a small town, and not much happens. When it does, people tend to remember."

Emma's heart sank. She rose to leave. "Well, thank you, Father, for your time." She had a sudden compulsion to leave the cozy little room and escape outside to feel the damp Irish mist on her face.

Father Michael rose, too, and accompanied her to the door. Emma gave him one of Mrs. Kelly's Danu House cards. "If you do find out anything, please call me at this number."

She stepped out onto the steps.

"Just a moment."

Emma turned to find Father Michael holding a camera in his hand.

"I'm sort of the parish photographer, and we don't get many visitors from America. Could I snap just one or two shots of you?"

An odd request, but an understandable one. Maybe he liked her face as much as she liked his.

"Sure," Emma said, putting her sadness aside and pulling her own camera out of her backpack. "As long as it's mutual."

And so Emma posed by the stone wall surrounding the church grounds for the County Meath parish priest. And he stood in front of his Gothic church for his portrait, a lonely if striking figure nearly lost in the morning mist.

CHAPTER SIXTEEN

"Do you think he'll help you?" asked Sam as they headed back to Dublin.

"He said he'd go through the records, whatever that means." Emma was suddenly tired; she was glad Sam was driving.

"Even if he finds something, would he tell you? I mean, aren't priests bound by a vow of confidentiality?"

"Yeah, but I liked him, and it seemed as if he liked me. I think he'll do what he can for me, if he *can* do anything." Emma looked at Sam. "What did you find?"

"Not much, I'm afraid." Sam pointed to the stack of photocopies on the seat between them. "County Meath is a pretty quiet place. The *Meath Chronicle* mostly covers local social and political activities—town meetings, weddings, funerals, births, stuff like that. Not a lot goes on in this town. And there's very little crime—all I found was the occasional pub fight."

"What about 1976 and 1977?"

"I photocopied the few interesting stories. There's a mugging or two, some vandalism, one murder, some tourist reports of strange sightings in the river Boyne, some domestic violence, and some problems with the gypsies. You can go through it for yourself when we get back to Danu House. Maybe you'll see something that I missed." Sam smiled at her. "You look exhausted. Try to nap now."

"Okay." Emma closed her eyes and tried to relax enough to sleep. But her overactive mind wouldn't rest. Something was fluttering there at the edge of her brain: something important, just out of reach. She concentrated, willing the thought to reveal itself. Nothing. She sighed, succumbing to her physical and emotional fatigue. She dozed off and dreamed of Father Michael. He sat before her, puffing contentedly on his pipe, surrounded by piles of files and folders.

Emma awoke with a start. "I've got it."

"Got what?" asked Sam, startled. "I thought you were asleep."

"I was." Emma leaned toward him, excited. "I remember now what Father Michael said about checking his records."

"What about it?"

"We've been operating all along under the assumption that my birth mother emigrated to America, and that I was born in America because that's what my birth certificate says."

"Dade County, City of Chicago."

"Right. But what if it's wrong? What if I was born right here in Ireland?"

"And they just changed the birth certificate." Sam thought about it. "Can they do that?"

"I don't know." Emma grinned. "But I'm going to find out."

After the drive back to Danu House, Emma and Sam sat down to another one of Mrs. Kelly's fantastic lunches. Then Sam and Emma parted ways. Sam took the car, heading back to County Meath to investigate the birth records there at the town hall.

Emma stayed behind in Dublin, where she planned to contact the Irish branch of ARN, Adoptive's Rights Now, dedicated to helping adoptive children find their birth parents. This was the same organization that Emma had worked with back home in Chicago to no avail. Though she had no paperwork to support her theory that she'd been born in Ireland, she could go ahead and check the place out. Besides, there was always the chance that her birth mother was trying to find her, just as she was searching for her birth mother. If so, she would have left word with ARN.

The ARN office was about ten blocks away; Emma would go on foot. She tucked ARN's address and Mrs. Kelly's directions into her backpack and prepared to leave. But just as she was about to go, Mrs. Kelly came up to her room.

"It's the telephone for you, Emma," she said, her eyebrows raised. "It's a young man. Not your Sam, either."

It must be Devin, Emma thought more happily than she should. She fought the urge to fly down the stairs, following Mrs. Kelly dutifully step by slow step. Mrs.

Kelly handed her the receiver, then left her alone in the parlor—although Emma could see it pained her to do so.

"Hello?" Emma asked, holding her breath.

"Miss America? Is that you?"

Emma laughed with relief. "Hi, Devin."

"I have a surprise for you."

"What sort of surprise?"

"You'll see. What are you doing this afternoon?"

"I was just on my way out for a walk."

"Great. Meet me at the Brazen Head on Bridge Street in an hour."

"Sam's not here," Emma said uncertainly, feeling disloyal in spite of herself. "He's gone for the afternoon."

"Then come without him. This surprise won't keep."

She wanted to see him, and she knew she might not get another chance—especially without Sam along. She could always go to the ARN office later, after seeing Devin. "Okay."

Devin gave her directions. "Don't worry, the Brazen Head is the oldest pub in Dublin. Everyone knows where it is. If you get lost, just ask anybody."

Emma loved the streets of Dublin. She walked the long way around to the Brazen Head, feeding the ducks on St. Stephen's Green, admiring the art in the store windows of the galleries of Temple Bar, wandering among the fruit and flower sellers of charming Moore Street, and finally hurrying past the old Guinness brewery to the Brazen Head on Bridge Street.

As much as she had enjoyed her walk, she was relieved to see the old seventeenth-century pub. She knew it was crazy, but she'd felt somewhat uneasy on the streets alone—as if there were some unnamed danger lurking among the friendly and cheerful faces of the Dubliners all around her. She couldn't shake the feeling that lingered from that morning at St. Peter's—the feeling that she was being watched. She made her way through the crowded pub, looking for Devin.

"There she is, Miss America," sang out a sardonic tenor behind her. Many of the pub's patrons nudged each other, grinning, as Devin serenaded her.

"Enough, enough," she said, feeling her face redden more with every note. Devin kissed her hand playfully, then escorted her through the lively throng to a small table at the back of the pub. There, with her back to Emma, sat a slender woman with shoulder-length auburn hair.

"This is my mother," Devin said by way of introduction. "Mama, this is Emma Lambourne, the girl I told you about."

The woman turned; to Emma's surprise she was Maeve Collins, the curator she'd spoken to at the National Museum. She stared at Emma in surprise and did not offer her hand. "We've met."

Devin looked at Emma for an explanation.

"At the museum," Emma said. "I can't believe you're Devin's mom!"

The woman smiled and regarded her son with obvious affection. "I can't believe it myself sometimes."

"So you already know that my mother is Ireland's foremost authority on the Celts," Devin said, his voice full of pride.

"How's your thesis coming?" Maeve asked Emma.

"What thesis?" Again Devin looked to Emma for an explanation.

"She's from the University of Chicago, where she's doing a thesis on Celtic arts," Maeve said before Emma could answer. "She didn't tell you that?"

"That's impossible. Sam said you were here on vacation."

"Who's Sam?" asked Maeve.

"Besides, you've just graduated from high school. You're not even in college yet."

Emma flushed. Like her mother always used to tell her, the trouble with lies was that they always caught up with you. How was she going to explain this? She sat there, her mind racing.

"Why would you lie?" asked Devin, more curious than angry.

"Because I couldn't tell you the truth," she blurted out, rising from her chair. "I'm so sorry," she said, grabbing her backpack. "I've got to go."

She rushed through the pub, jostling patrons and apologizing as she went. Once outside, she leaned against the old stone front of the building. Tears stung her eyes. She was ashamed of herself. She knew she should go back in and explain herself, but she didn't know what to say. If she told them about the gold owl piece, Maeve would expect her to give it to the museum. She couldn't do that—not just yet. Maybe when this was all over, when she'd found out who she was and where the other half of the bracelet was, maybe then she and Devin could be friends again.

She started back to Danu House with a heavy heart. It was going to be a long, lonely walk.

Emma was within a block of Danu House when it happened. Lost in painful thoughts of her embarrassing encounter with Devin and his mother, she trudged along, her backpack heavy on her spine, her eyes on the cobblestones beneath her.

She felt so demoralized. She was spending all her time and all her money on this search, but she was going nowhere. What had she accomplished? And at what price? She'd never be able to afford to go to Brooks now; to finance her education she'd have to sell the only home she'd ever known. She'd lied to people who'd trusted her, nice people. Worse, she'd put Sam in danger, after all he'd done for her during the past few terrible months. What was the matter with her? What difference did it make where she came from if she didn't like who she was now?

Suddenly something hit her hard from behind. She lurched forward. Her feet came out from under her and her arms were twisted back as she felt her backpack being ripped from her shoulders. She was falling, falling toward a swirl of cobblestones. Instinctively, she tried to push her arms out in front of her to break her fall. But whatever, whoever, was holding them back did not release them until it was too late. Desperately she jerked her head to the right to spare her face, and slammed into the sidewalk.

Emma stood alone in the middle of the central domed chamber of Newgrange. It was dark and damp. A thick black mist hung in the chamber, obscuring the exits. Emma couldn't see anything, but she knew that someone, something, was after her. She had to get out of there.

She inched forward, groping for the stone walls. Finally her grasping hands met the cold stone. She traced the spiral patterns cut into the walls with her fingers, feeling for an opening leading out of the chamber. Finally she found such an opening and, shuddering with relief, slipped into the long narrow passage, intent on escape.

But escape did not come. The long, dark tunnel led only to another, then another, and another. Caught in a maze, Emma ran blindly down one slim underground artery, only to find herself in another. She could feel her enemies gathering at her back, but she couldn't see who they were or even what they were. She panicked, running faster and faster, going deeper and deeper into the maze.

Breathing hard, she stumbled through the next passageway, which seemed somehow even longer and narrower than the others. The stone walls were closing in on her; their carved spirals swam before her eyes. She heard the rustle of her pursuers behind her, haunting her every step. The rustling grew louder and louder, until the eerie noise became the shrieking of banshees. Then the great wailing enveloped her, and she too began to scream and scream and scream.

"Emma!"

She heard her name called as if the sound had been hurled through a tunnel, echoing fiercely in her brain.

Her head ached. She closed her eyes against the pain as someone cradled her in strong arms.

"Emma!"

The voice was very close now, and familiar. Emma opened her eyes to the handsome face of the Irish boy she'd liked and lied to, Devin O'Connor.

"Oh, Devin, I'm so—"

"Don't talk. You have suffered a concussion, no doubt."

"I don't understand. Where did you come from?"

"I wanted to talk to you, so I drove round to Danu House to see you. I was standing outside and saw you coming. I saw the guy attack you. I tried to stop him but—"

"It all happened so fast."

"Shh. He stole your backpack." Devin touched the sore spot on Emma's head.

"Ouch."

"It's a nasty knot, I'm afraid." Devin looked at her with concern. "We need to get you to the hospital now." He helped her to her feet, then lifted her easily into his arms.

"I can walk," Emma protested mildly.

"Be quiet now." Devin lifted her into a waiting cab and deposited her gently on the backseat. He moved in next to her, laying her head carefully in his lap.

She stared up at him as he told the cabbie where to go. *What a great guy,* she thought, right before she drifted out of consciousness once again.

Emma opened her eyes, and there he was again.

"Feeling better, Miss America?" Devin leaned over her, his dark, wavy hair falling over his forehead.

Emma tried to smile but winced instead. "My head hurts," she admitted. "Something hit me. ... " She couldn't remember. Her mind seemed to be running in slow motion.

"Don't move. The doctor says you have a slight concussion."

She looked beyond Devin for the first time. She was on an examining table under a sheet in what appeared to be Ireland's version of a hospital emergency room. She was relieved to realize she still wore her clothes, although someone had unbuttoned her shirt and removed her shoes and socks. She hoped it had been a nurse. She looked at Devin, blushing.

But it was no time for false modesty, she chided herself. She had to think. "Where's my vest?"

"What?" Devin regarded her with a blank look.

"My vest." She tried to sit up, but her head swam with dark clouds and she was forced to lie back once again.

"Keep still," Devin scolded. "Your vest is right over there on that chair." He pointed to the obligatory plastic guest chair. "It was your backpack they stole, not the vest."

"Oh." Emma was relieved; the owl piece was not in her backpack. "Good."

"What do you mean, good?" Devin stared at her. "What about that camera you're so devoted to?"

"Oh, no, my camera!" In her concern for the owl piece she'd completely forgotten about her camera. Flustered,

Emma tried to explain. "I forgot about my camera. It was in there. I've had it out most of the time I've been here."

There was a knock at the door; a police officer poked his head in. "Miss Lambourne?" he asked.

"Come in," Emma said. The police officer, a congenial-looking young man with a shock of carrot-red hair, introduced himself as Sergeant Danny O'Donnell. He held Emma's backpack in one hand.

"You found it?"

"About six blocks from where you were attacked. We'd like to know what was taken."

"Sure." Before she could reach for it, Devin took the backpack from the sergeant and set it carefully on her lap.

"I'll go through it for you, okay? Don't move."

"How's my camera?" Emma held her breath as Devin carefully removed the clutter of items: her Dublin guidebook, some postcards, an apple, extra film and batteries, and her beloved camera.

"My camera." Emma's eyes suddenly filled with tears. She reached for it, and Devin placed it in her open hands. She ran her fingers over its controls and sighed with relief. "I think it'll still work." She gazed up at the police officer. "It's a good camera. I can't believe they didn't take it."

Sergeant O'Donnell shrugged. "Is anything missing?"

"I don't think so."

"You carried no money or traveler's checks or any such valuables?" the sergeant asked.

"Not in my backpack. Just my camera." She grinned. "Maybe they hate having their picture taken."

"Maybe." The sergeant seemed unconvinced. "Did you see who did this?"

Emma shook her head. "They came up from behind me. I really don't know what happened."

"Mr. O'Connor here gave me a description of the man who jumped you, along with that of a suspicious-looking man who could have been an accomplice." He handed Emma a card. "If we catch the perpetrators, we'll be in touch. You're staying at Danu House, is that right?"

Emma nodded.

"If you remember anything, contact me," he said, indicating the card in her hand, and left.

Devin replaced her things in the backpack and zipped it shut. Then he put it down on the floor next to her bed.

"How long do I have to stay here?" Emma's head was beginning to clear; she felt better.

"They want to keep you here for the night, to rest."

"I can rest at Danu House. Mrs. Kelly will take good care of me."

"You're a stubborn girl, I can see that," Devin said with a quick grin. Then his grin faded, and a frown took its place. "But you aren't going anywhere until you tell me what happened at the Brazen Head."

Emma could see by the set of Devin's strong jaw that he was serious. She was going to have to tell him the truth; she owed him that much.

"It's a long story," she warned him. She'd been saying that a lot lately. She'd spent much of her time in the Emerald Isle telling these long stories of hers. *Thank goodness the Irish love stories,* she thought.

"I've got all night," Devin said, pulling up the plastic chair and settling into it. "Do go on."

Emma took a deep breath. *Here goes nothing,* she thought. She looked Devin straight in the eye and said, "I came to Ireland to find my mother."

CHAPTER SEVENTEEN

Mary spent the months after Michael left for the seminary planning her escape to America. She would sit on the damp stone wall by the holy well for hours, inventing an elaborate future for herself. At first, confident that Michael would return to her momentarily, Mary's strategies were little more than daydreams, in which she and Michael sold the owl bracelet to finance a wonderful new life in America. She pictured the two of them in the fabulous places they'd read about together—a cabin in the Rockies, or a plantation in the South, or a shack on a beach in Hawaii. But as the days passed without even a postcard from Michael, Mary realized that he was not coming back. So she adapted her fantasies to the hard realities of her life.

Her thoughts drifted to Sean Leahy, a local boy who wanted to marry her. He was a nice enough boy, good-looking, too. But he wasn't Michael and he never would be. Sean had a cousin in America who had prospered there. He owned a pub in Boston now and promised Sean a partnership should he emigrate.

Mary could have sold her half of the bracelet and gone to America on her own, but she simply couldn't bring herself to do it. It was the superstitious gypsy in her, she supposed. If she sold off her half of the bracelet, she sold off her dream of finding true happiness with Michael. The bracelet was all she had left of him. Life was long, she thought, and anything could happen. She didn't want to hex what little chance she had of marrying her one true love.

That day, however, she felt more like cursing Michael than marrying him. She sat in her usual place at the holy well, her long bare legs dangling off the edge of the stone wall, her toes tickling the cold water below.

Sean was leaving for America by New Year's. He was resolved to go, he'd told her just the day before—with or without her.

Michael had wasted nearly a year of his life at that seminary; it appeared he was ready to waste the rest of it there, too. "I'm not spending another year of my life waiting for you," she said aloud, kicking at the well water with her feet. Her stepfather was getting drunker and meaner by the day; she didn't like the way he looked at her when her mother wasn't around. She didn't know how much longer she could stay at home. It was time to stop daydreaming about her ghost lover and get on with her future. Sean was a good man who'd take good care of her—at least until she got to America, a progressive place where a smart girl could learn to take care of herself.

And she *was* smart; Michael had said so, and he was the smartest person she'd ever met.

Michael again. She shook her head, auburn hair flying, scolding herself for even thinking about him. She pulled her wet legs up out of the water and scrambled to her feet. She crossed herself quickly, in acknowledgment of the sacred nature of the holy well, and turned to go.

"Michael," she whispered, catching sight of a shadowy figure in the mist. The tall figure dissolved into the gray gloom. *Pathetic girl,* she told herself, *seeing your beloved in the shadows. Better get yourself to America before you start seeing the faery people.*

She walked on through the early morning fog, which grew thicker with each step. She'd have to do something about her constant daydreaming about Michael. Maybe her mother could cast a spell on her to chase his haunting ghost away from her mind.

She heard a rustling behind her and stopped to listen. She'd slipped out of the house unnoticed while her stepfather was sleeping off his hangover, or so she thought. But she wouldn't be surprised if he'd followed her out there. Silently she retrieved the pocketknife she carried in her skirt pocket. If he touched her, she'd kill him.

She couldn't see anything; the fog was so thick she couldn't see her own hand if she held it out in front of her. She remained perfectly still, listening for whomever was out there, waiting for him to reveal himself.

Another rustle, and he was upon her. She flicked open her knife as his strong arms turned her around to face him. As he pulled her to him she clutched the knife, ready to strike. His lips found hers.

"Oh, Mary," he said. At the sound of his voice, she dropped the knife.

It was Michael. She didn't know why he was there, or if he would stay, but she didn't care. Either way, she wanted him. She had to know what she would be missing if she had to live without him.

She drew away from him. Taking his hand, she led him back through the mist to the damp stone wall of the holy well.

CHAPTER EIGHTEEN

"How could you do it?" Sam was angrier than Emma had ever seen him.

"He may have saved my life," Emma told him. She was still in the hospital, now in a private room. The doctor had insisted that she stay overnight for observation. She could leave in the morning.

Alerted by Mrs. Kelly, Sam had come over to see her as soon as he returned from Navan. He'd burst into the room just as she was showing Devin the gold owl piece hidden in the chest pocket of her photographer's vest.

"What the hell are you doing?" he'd said, glaring at Devin, who excused himself promptly.

He calmed down long enough to make sure she was all right, but he was still upset. "You don't know anything about this guy."

"That's not true. I know a lot about him. I even met his mother."

"What?" Sam stared at her.

"I met his mother today—and you won't believe who she is." Emma waited for Sam to ask. But he simply crossed his arms across his chest and stood there next to her bed in a stony silence. "She's the curator at the National Museum, the one I talked to."

"I don't care if she's the president of Ireland," Sam said. "We said we weren't going to tell anybody about the owl. You promised."

"Things change, Sam. Under the circumstances—"

"Under the circumstances," Sam said, his voice low and tight, "you don't know whether he tried to save you or rob you."

"Don't be ridiculous." Emma was growing angry herself. Her head ached, and with every word Sam was making it ache all the more.

"Don't you find it a little *too* coincidental that you've had all this trouble since you met this guy? *And* his mother?"

"I can't believe you, Sam. This is so unlike you, to be so—so petty."

"I am not being petty. I'm only asking you to think rationally about what has happened here." Sam's voice was gentler now. He took her hand.

Emma pulled her hand away; she wasn't ready to forgive him just yet. "You're jealous, Sam, and I don't like it."

"Now who's being ridiculous?" Sam walked away from the bed, then turned toward Emma. He ran his fingers through his sandy hair in frustration. "Don't you understand, Emma? I'm worried about you. If anything happened to you ... " His voice trailed off.

"I understand that when it comes to Devin, you're crazy. Here he practically saved my life, and—"

"It should have been *me,* Emma. I should never have left you alone." Sam hung his head.

"Sam, it's not your fault." Emma sighed. "Don't be so macho. I can take care of myself. I don't need you to be my bodyguard; I need you to be my friend."

Sam looked at her. "I'm more than your friend. I love you, Emma. You know that. I came here to help you find out whatever you need to know to get on with your life. Your life back home in Chicago." He didn't say, "with me," but Emma knew he was thinking it.

"I can't think that far ahead, not yet."

He took her hands in his. "Maybe it's time we go back there," he said gently. "While we still can."

"I'm not going anywhere, Sam."

"It's too dangerous to stay, can't you see that?"

"I'm not leaving until I've tried everything."

"Whoever did this to you will try again. The next time they could kill you."

"I'm fine. I'm going to stay and do what I can to find out who I am. You can stay with me, or you can go on home. It's up to you."

"How can you say that?" Sam released her hands. "Unless that's the way you want it."

Emma didn't know what she wanted. Her head throbbed; all she wanted was to be left alone. She leaned back against the hard hospital pillow and closed her eyes. She was not going to beg him to stay.

"I guess that says it all. You have Devin to take care of you. I guess I shouldn't worry."

Emma didn't say anything. She was so confused—about Sam, about Devin, about what to do next.

"I love you, Emma." Sam leaned over and kissed her gently on the forehead. "I hope you find what you're looking for."

"Good-bye, Sam." Emma willed herself not to cry. She knew he'd stay if she asked him to, but she didn't want to hurt him any more than she already had. She needed some time to figure things out first. She opened her eyes to catch a last glimpse of Sam—but he was already gone.

By the time Devin escorted Emma back to Danu House the next day, Sam had checked out.

"He packed up his things last night and left," a distressed Mrs. Kelly informed her. "I tried to tell him that the cards said he should stay, but he wouldn't listen." Mrs. Kelly lowered her voice so Devin couldn't hear her. "He was very hurt, my dear. He loves you very much."

"Too much," Emma said. Maybe she wasn't ready for anyone to love her. It bound her too tightly, demanded too much in return. The only person who had ever really loved her was her mother, Grace, and she was gone. And now Sam was gone as well. Love hurt too much.

To avoid the irrepressible Mrs. Kelly's questions, Emma excused herself and went upstairs to change into some clean jeans.

"I'll wait down here," Devin said, "and chat with Mrs. Kelly."

But when Emma came back downstairs some fifteen minutes later, Devin was gone.

"Where's Devin?"

"He got a phone call and left right away," Mrs. Kelly said. "You seem to be scaring off young men everywhere you go today." She handed Emma a slip of paper.

"Very funny," Emma told her, and proceeded to read the note from Devin. It said that his mother had called him away on a family emergency.

"I hope everything's okay," Emma told Mrs. Kelly, after explaining to her what the note said.

"You should be worried about yourself, my dear." Mrs. Kelly pointed to the small bandage that still covered her bruised head. "The young men have gone now and you are alone. I am an old woman, I can do only so much. Who will protect you?"

"Don't be so old-fashioned," Emma told her, exasperation coloring her voice. "I can take care of myself." She seemed to be saying that a lot lately.

"But the cards say you must be careful."

"I will be." She headed back upstairs again. "I won't be going out until after lunch. And I promise to be back by dark, okay?"

Mrs. Kelly shook her head. "You are a stubborn child," she chided.

Upstairs, in the privacy of her room, Emma lay down on the bed and stared up at the ceiling. "What am I doing here?" she asked herself aloud. "Am I crazy?" Maybe Sam was right. Maybe she should leave right away—before she really did get hurt. She'd already alienated Sam and squandered most of her inheritance. She touched the bandage on her forehead and winced. She'd been lucky so far, lucky to keep the owl and herself intact. She removed it from the inside pocket of her vest and stared at it. So *beautiful,* she thought. *And so compelling. My mother, Grace, wanted me to have this and she wanted me to use it to find out who I am.* Emma's eyes filled with tears at the thought of the woman who had loved her so much she was willing to step aside and take second place in her daughter's heart so that she would never be without a family.

Oh, Mama, she thought, tears now streaming down her cheeks, *no one could* ever *replace you.* Emma looked again at the gold owl piece, her mother's promise that she would never be alone.

She owed it to her mother—and to herself—to try and fulfill that promise. *I'll give the search twenty-four more hours,* she told herself. *If I don't find out anything, I'll go home.*

There was no time to waste. Emma replaced the gold piece and set to work. She considered what she'd learned so far. She had the stack of news clippings Sam had gathered from the *Meath Chronicle,* along with his notes from the records authority and the prints from the dozens of rolls of film she'd taken since her trip began. She spread it all out on the bed before her, sorted through it, and put to one side the most intriguing materials. Using the tape and scissors from the desk drawer, she cut out clippings and images and records and stuck them to the back of her door, hoping that something would occur to her. It made an interesting collage, but … There were the photos she'd taken out at Newgrange, which she arranged as Father Michael had arranged his; the news clippings about the strange sightings of ghosts and faeries reported by tourists; a crusade by the local city council to drive out the gypsies for gambling, public drunkenness, and disorderly conduct; the murder—or was it suicide?—of a County Meath spinster; two reports of domestic violence; the records naming the dozens of babies born in County Meath within three months of Emma's birthday—fifty-three girls, fifty-seven boys, and two sets of twins; and the literature about ancient Celtic tongues she'd gotten from the National Museum.

The door was now carefully papered, a complete accounting of everything Emma had learned about the circumstances of her birth since arriving in Ireland—a scrambled collection of puzzle pieces. All she had to do was put them together. The trouble was, she didn't know which belonged to the puzzle and which didn't. Her eyes on the door, she backed up to the bed and sat down. She sat there for a long time, staring at the collage before her, wondering what it could tell her, if only she knew how to read it.

After lunch Emma went to the ARN office. It was a small, one-room operation, consisting of a couple of desks, a bank of file cabinets, and a computer system. A woman named Moira helped her fill out the paperwork.

"What a coincidence," Moira said as she looked over Emma's information sheets. "We had a couple in here just yesterday from County Meath. They were looking for a daughter about your age."

Emma grew excited in spite of herself. "Really?"

"Let me get their file." Moira retrieved a new folder from her in-box. "I haven't even gotten around to filing this case yet." She consulted the information sheet. "I was right," she told Emma with a smile. "The Brennans say their baby girl, Erin Bridget, was born at County Meath Hospital on May fifth eighteen years ago."

"Brennan," repeated Emma, thinking back to the birth records hanging on her hotel room door. "They were on the list." She filled Moira in on her data-gathering efforts.

"This is very encouraging," Moira said. "When's your birthday?"

"My American birth certificate says May fifteenth." Emma showed her the certificate.

Moira smiled again. "*Very* encouraging. Let me do some checking, and if it works out, we'll arrange a meeting."

Late that afternoon Moira called to say she had great news. She'd contacted the Brennans, and they'd agreed to a meeting the next morning.

"Everything appears to check out. This could be it," she told Emma. "Good luck."

CHAPTER NINETEEN

May 10, 1994

Dear Sally,

I don't know where to begin. So much has happened in the past forty-eight hours. I have never been more confused, scared, or excited in my life.

Let me explain....

I'm confused because I met this guy—the guy I told you about in the postcard I sent you from Newgrange. He's like no guy I've ever met before. He's very cute, and Irish, of course, but it's more than that. I know this sounds crazy, but I feel as if I've known him forever. I feel so connected to him, so drawn to him—why, I'm not even sure. He can be very brash—even obnoxious at times. I can just see you jumping up and down now yelling, "What about Sam? What about Sam?"

The truth is, Sam left. By the time you read this, he'll probably already be home in Chicago. He's jealous of Devin—though there's really no reason for him to be, since Devin and I are just friends, and brand-new friends at that. I love Sam, but he wants more from me than I can give him. He wants—and deserves—a girl who can give as much to their relationship as he does. I just can't do that—not now, maybe not ever. He wanted me to go home with him.

Which brings me to scared. Whoever went through our luggage didn't stop there. They mugged me, stealing my backpack and knocking me down in the process. The owl piece is safe, and I'm fine except for a slight concussion. Sam's worried that they'll really hurt me next time. Knowing you, you probably agree with him. Don't jump on the next plane, though. I want to give this search of mine twenty-four hours more. If I don't find anything, I'm out of here.

But I just may find out the truth tomorrow, which is why I'm so excited. At the local ARN office here in Dublin I learned about the Brennans, a couple looking for the daughter they gave up. We're about the same age, and this baby was born in County Meath, where the owl torque comes from and where I believe I was born. Of course, it's a long shot, but still...

I've got to go now; tomorrow is a big day and I need my rest. Wish me luck.

Love,
Emma

P. S. No worrying!

Emma signed her letter to Sally with a flourish and then prepared for her appointment with the Brennans. The meeting was to take place in the Brennans' home in the prestigious southside suburb of Dublin known as Ballsbridge.

"Quite posh," Mrs. Kelly had told her. "You'd do best to wear a frock, dear."

She had brought only one dress with her, a simple shift of pale green silk. Sally had chosen it for her, saying it set off her auburn hair and green eyes.

Emma eyed herself critically in the mirror. She'd let her hair down and applied a little blush, mascara, and lip gloss. She supposed she looked presentable enough, but wished Sally were there to make sure.

She was nervous. She ran a brush through her hair for the umpteenth time, then tossed it aside. She might as well go right away; she wasn't going to look any better than she did already, no matter how long she fussed.

"Very pretty," Mrs. Kelly said approvingly when Emma came downstairs.

"Thank you. Is my hair all right now?"

"Just lovely." Mrs. Kelly regarded Emma with concern. "But I don't think you should go alone."

"I'll be fine."

"I would be glad to accompany you."

"That won't be necessary." Emma gave Mrs. Kelly a kiss on the cheek. "I appreciate it, but this is something I need to do alone."

Once on the road, Emma had second thoughts about her solitary journey. Driving along the Northumberland

Road she twice suspected she was being followed; both times the cars turned off the road, not to return again. Still, Emma was somewhat shaken. She missed Sam. She hadn't realized until then just how much she depended on him. He was the one person in the world she could count on, and she'd pushed him away. She promised herself to make it up to him when she got home.

If she got home. Emma shivered. For the first time she was really scared. She gripped the steering wheel to steady herself. She wondered why she hadn't been frightened before, considering all that had happened to her.

That question had an easy answer, she realized. Before, she'd had Sam. Now Sam was gone, and she was scared.

She checked her directions; she was nearly there. At the next crossroads she turned left; a few blocks later she parked the car in the circular drive of an elegant Georgian estate.

She didn't get out of the car right away. She sat there, thinking of Grace Lambourne, the woman who had raised her, the woman she called Mama. Now she would walk into the grand home before her, possibly to meet her other Mama, the woman who had given her life.

"Thank you," she said aloud to Grace Lambourne. "I will love you forever."

With that, Emma exited the car and approached the house. Taking a deep breath, she rang the doorbell. The bright red door opened almost immediately, revealing an attractive couple in their late forties.

"Hello." Emma extended her hand to the petite woman before her. "I'm Emma Lambourne."

The woman smiled and clasped Emma's hand warmly. "I'm Irene Brennan and this is my husband, Patrick. Do come in."

Emma shook Mr. Brennan's hand as well and then followed them through a marble-floored entry to a formal sitting room filled with expensive antiques. Oddly enough, the handsomely appointed room could have been straight out of Kenilworth.

The three of them settled into two plump chintz loveseats flanking the carved mahogany fireplace, Emma on one and the Brennans on the other. A tea table stood between them, set for high tea.

Emma regarded them with interest. Tastefully dressed in a pastel pink suit, Mrs. Brennan was a sweet-faced woman with graying red curls and pale gray eyes. She smiled a lot, and fingered with tiny freckled hands the pearls she wore around her neck. Mr. Brennan was a tall, beefy man with a ruddy complexion and a ready twinkle in his bright blue eyes. He wore an expensively tailored navy suit with a starched white shirt and a red silk tie.

Emma had expected a sudden surge of recognition, as if her soul would know immediately if these two nice people were her birth parents. An unrealistic expectation, she knew, but she couldn't help but feel disappointed somehow.

"You look just like my grandmother," Mrs. Brennan said, staring at Emma. "The same beautiful hair, the same perfect skin, the same high cheekbones."

Emma was a little taken aback. The woman had only just met her, and she was already talking as if Emma were the one, the daughter she'd never known.

"Yes," Mr. Brennan agreed. "The image of your grandmother."

"I must show you our album," Mrs. Brennan said, starting to rise.

"Now, Irene." Her husband placed a thick hand on the petite woman's thin shoulders. "I'm sure Emma—may I call you Emma?—has some questions she'd like to ask us first."

"Of course." Mrs. Brennan sank down onto the couch again as lightly as a feather. Her pale hands fluttered to her lap. "Do excuse me, dear, I'm just so excited. ... " Her high voice trailed off.

"Why don't you pour, Irene?" Mr. Brennan directed his wife, then turned to Emma. "What would you like to know?"

"I'd like to know how you met," Emma answered quietly, hoping they could tell her something that would help her decide if they were her parents or not.

"Of course." He cleared his throat. "It was nearly twenty years ago now, though I remember it as if it were yesterday. We met at a church social. Irene wore a blue dress. She was dancing with another man. I cut in."

Mrs. Brennan handed Emma her tea. "Patrick was the most handsome man I'd ever seen. So tall and striking."

"We were inseparable after that," he said, taking his wife's hand.

"We were to be married in the spring," his wife said. "But then the Troubles stirred up again."

"I was young and hotheaded," Mr. Brennan said. "I joined the IRA, a rebel with a noble cause. I went out on a mission—"

"We thought he was lost, you see," interjected Mrs. Brennan. "They said he was dead."

"I had to leave the country," he added. "I couldn't tell anyone I was alive."

"By this time I was expecting," Mrs. Brennan said, looking away from Emma. "I didn't know what to do. My family pressured me to give the baby up for adoption. They sent me off to County Meath to stay until the baby was born." She wiped tiny tears from the corners of her eyes with her linen tea napkin. "I had a girl, a beautiful baby girl I named Erin Bridget. But my parents made me give you up. I was so young and so frightened. ..." The woman dissolved into tears. Her husband put his arm around her protectively and continued the story for her.

"I never knew about the baby, not until I came back two years later. By then it was too late. We married at once and have prayed together every day that we would find you."

"Then why did you wait so long to go to ARN?" Emma asked.

"We were waiting for you to grow up, to reach your eighteenth birthday," Mr. Brennan explained. "We didn't feel it would be fair to your adoptive parents to contact ARN any sooner."

"We would never have forced ourselves on you," Mrs. Brennan added. "We didn't want to hurt you in any way."

They regarded Emma with great tenderness and love.

"You really believe I'm the one," Emma said, not knowing what to think.

"Oh, yes. We are so happy to have found you," Mrs. Brennan said.

"We never had any other children, you know." Mr. Brennan smiled at her. "You can see how happy we are."

They were so sweet, so sincere. Emma smiled back. Though she had experienced no psychic soul connection to these people, she did feel very close to them—much closer than she should after knowing them only twenty minutes. They obviously cared for each other and for the baby they'd never known—her.

Mrs. Brennan excused herself to retrieve the family album.

"She's never forgiven herself for giving you up," Mr. Brennan told Emma after his wife left the room. "Now maybe she can find some peace."

Mrs. Brennan returned with a handsome leather volume. "May I?" she asked, sitting down next to Emma. She opened the album and flipped through the first few pages. "Here she is," she said, pointing to an old black-and-white portrait of an elegant young woman dressed in twenties-style clothes. "My grandmother, Deirdre."

Emma stared at the picture. There was a resemblance, she could see it—something about the woman's bone structure that recalled her own face. Emma stared harder. And as she stared a frozen piece of her heart broke away and melted into tears. She looked up into the pale gray eyes of Mrs. Brennan, and began to cry.

CHAPTER TWENTY

Mary stripped off her shirt and skirt and slipped naked into the well. It was a shallow pool, not much deeper than a bathtub, but the cool waters soothed her body and soul nonetheless. She drifted in the water, her thoughts drifting along with her body to the inevitable subject: Michael. After their one magical afternoon together at the holy well, he had gone back to the seminary and Mary had agreed to marry Sean.

She had made peace with her plans and herself. Michael was not hers, and never would be. She might as well accept that and get on with her life.

So she and Sean had arranged to go to America. Mary had taken a job as a waitress in the local pub to save money for the trip while Sean studied for his bartender's license.

These preparations had helped Mary banish Michael from her head, if not her heart. She had managed to keep her conscious thoughts of Michael at bay, but still he appeared nightly to haunt her dreams. She had struggled to program her subconscious to eliminate him from her dreams, but to no avail. Finally, in desperation, she had asked her mother to cast a spell upon her dreams for her. That had seemed to work.

But just about the time Mary had stopped dreaming about Michael, she had realized she was carrying his child. This realization had rocked her to her core. What was she going to do?

She'd gone to the holy well that day to think. She had not been there since that afternoon with Michael. She continued to float aimlessly in the well, her bare toes splashing. The right thing to do was ... what? She kicked at the water in frustration. Some would say Michael had a right to know; it was his child, too, after all. But others would say to render unto God what was God's, and spare Michael the pain of the truth. Mary knew some women would simply bed Sean and let him believe the baby was his—but she could never do that. There was only one thing she could do. She was nothing if not honest.

A wave of nausea hit her, followed by a rush of heat. Mary sighed, placing her hand over her womb. She held her breath until the nausea passed, then exhaled slowly. She floated there for a long time, enjoying the peace and quiet. It was the last peace and quiet she was to have for a while, and she knew it.

Dear Michael,

I am writing you this letter because I believe you have the right to know the truth.

The truth is, I'm pregnant. The baby is yours. I know you are due to take your vows soon. If you choose to leave the seminary and come home to me and your baby, I will be waiting for you. If you do not, I will go ahead and marry Sean Leahy—if he'll still have me.

Of course, I love you and always will.

Love,
Mary

Michael never answered her letter. The months went by; pretty soon she wouldn't be able to hide her condition any longer. Her mother had already guessed, thanks to the revelations of her beloved tarot cards. And her stepfather was beginning to suspect something was wrong as well. No doubt he'd throw her out of the house when he figured out the truth.

The worst part was telling Sean. Sean truly loved her, and she hated to hurt him. But tell him she did. And he responded exactly the way she had predicted he would. He raised his hand to strike her, then dropped his arm and walked away without a word. She hadn't seen him since. She continued to work in the pub, but Sean never went in there anymore. She saved her money and prayed for a miracle.

She often slipped away to the holy well to soak her tired legs, worn out both from the strain of pregnancy and from being on her feet all night at the pub.

As her pregnancy progressed she needed the long soaks more than ever. So she would leave the house early, before her stepfather woke from his drunken sleep, even before her mother was up. Fortunately, he had not yet guessed her condition. If she dressed carefully and avoided him, she might be able to deceive him a little while longer.

She went to the well one day when it was cool and quiet—a soft day full of mist, much like the day when Michael had come to her. Mary removed her clothes and sank into the well water. She loved being naked in the water now, where she could stroke her swelling belly and talk to her baby in complete privacy. She told her baby stories, the same stories Michael had told her. That day she recited the sad story of Blathnait, the Flower Daughter, her quiet voice echoing softly through the well.

"And so Blathnait was transformed into an owl," she told her baby. "The Lady of the Night. And she roamed the skies from dusk to dawn every night, looking for her lost love, Cu Chulainn, calling, *'Cu cu cu.'* "

"Cu cu cu!" came a familiar voice from behind her.

Mary froze, then sank deeper into the water, so that only her head and neck remained above the surface of the pool. Slowly she turned to meet the voice, her body still submerged.

Michael stood at the edge of the stone wall, Mary's clothes at his feet. "Marry," he said.

"Michael," she answered.

"It's good to see you again," he said with a gentle look in his eyes.

Mary said nothing.

"I've missed you so much. More than I could possibly have imagined I could. I should never have left you like I did. Please forgive me."

"There's nothing to forgive," Mary said quietly. "You did what you had to do. And now I will do what I have to do."

Michael regarded her uncertainly. "What do you mean?"

"You should have answered my letter, you know," Mary went on. "That would have been the proper thing to do."

Michael gave her a blank look. "What letter?"

Mary stared at him. "Then you don't know?"

Michael squatted down at the edge of the stone wall so he could see Mary better through the mist. "Know what?"

He was so close to her now that she could practically reach up and touch him. But she didn't touch him. Mary simply rose out of the water like Botticelli's Venus, her lithe, fertile body glistening in the gloom like a beacon.

"Sweet Jesus," whispered Michael.

CHAPTER TWENTY-ONE

Emma stayed with the Brennans until dinnertime, going through the family album and crying and talking—trying to cover the space of eighteen years in a few short hours.

"I'd better go now," she told them reluctantly when she realized it was nearly six o'clock. "Mrs. Kelly is expecting me."

"Do you have to go?" asked Mrs. Brennan.

Emma gave her a hug. "It's been an emotional day for all of us."

"You will join us for luncheon tomorrow?" Mr. Brennan asked.

"We have so much more to talk about," Mrs. Brennan added.

"Of course," Emma reassured them.

They accompanied her to the door, where they each kissed her good-bye on the cheek.

"Tomorrow, then," said Mrs. Brennan anxiously.

"Tomorrow," answered Emma with a smile.

She'd driven maybe five miles before she realized she'd never even asked them about the owl piece. And they had never asked her about it, either. Maybe they were waiting for a more appropriate time. First things first, after all. Either way, she'd ask them about it the next day.

She drove on, her mind on the Brennans rather than the road. The whole time she'd spent with them seemed so unreal. Had she really just met her parents? Distracted, she screeched to a stop just inches from a stalled truck. Unnerved by the near miss, she turned off at a roadside pub just down the road. She parked in the back, then went inside for a strong cup of tea. She sat in front by the window and stared out at nothing. The day's dramatic events had drained her; she felt numb. She sipped her tea and tried to digest everything that had happened that day. She sat there for quite a while; she was on her third cup of tea when she noticed the Brennans out in front of the pub. Leaning against the grille of their blue Mercedes, they were obviously waiting for someone. Emma considered going out to greet them, but thought better of it. She'd see them again the next day, when she was more herself.

A black Rolls-Royce pulled up next to the Brennans' Mercedes. A tall, distinguished-looking man got out and approached the Brennans.

To Emma's surprise, she recognized the man immediately. It was Mr. Archer, the cosmopolitan gentleman she had met on the plane.

He shook hands with each of the Brennans, then they huddled together in deep conversation. Emma wondered what they were talking about—and how they could possibly know each other.

What a coincidence ... if it *was* a coincidence. Emma jerked open her backpack and retrieved a pen and notebook just as Mr. Archer handed Mr. Brennan an envelope. Then they started back to their respective cars. Emma wrote down their license plate numbers before they drove away in opposite directions.

She waited for half an hour before leaving the pub, just to make sure she wouldn't encounter either vehicle on the road. Then she drove straight home to Danu House, one nervous eye on the rearview mirror.

There were three messages for her when she returned: one from Devin, one from the Brennans, and one from Father Michael. There was no message from Sam.

She didn't know who to call first, so she didn't call anybody. She just ate Mrs. Kelly's fine supper, fended off her many questions, pleaded a headache, and went to bed early, where she dreamed of her mother, Grace.

"The Magician is the Archdruid," Mrs. Kelly said, pointing to the card with the berobed priest encircled by the great symbols of the Celts: the swords, the wands, and the cauldron of eternity. "The wisest and most powerful of the Druid priests, capable of great magic. You must not be fooled by the Archdruid's tricks," she warned cryptically.

It was the next morning, and Mrs. Kelly had insisted on reading Emma's tarot cards before she left for the day, saying, "You mustn't go off unprepared."

They sat together at the tea table, which Mrs. Kelly had covered with a piece of Irish lace. Emma had chosen three cards from the circle Mrs. Kelly had spread before her. The Archdruid was the first. The second was the Chariot.

"The Chariot is a card of action," Mrs. Kelly said, tapping the picture of the brave warrior charging into battle in his horse-drawn chariot. "The charioteer is Cu Chulainn, the Celtic hero who faced many formidable foes. This card tells you to 'know thine enemies.'" Mrs. Kelly looked up at Emma, her eyes bright with anxiety. "You must be cautious, my dear. Trust no one."

That would be easy, Emma thought, especially after what had happened the day before.

Mrs. Kelly turned to the last card with relief. "This is the Hierophant, the spirited seeker and mystic. It's a strong card with a strong message, the archetype of the willow tree. The willow tree was sacred to the ancient Celts, empowered with the gifts of enchantment and mystical vision. You must listen and learn from all you experience today. Think with your heart, your mind, and your soul—and you will succeed."

Emma thanked Mrs. Kelly and retreated to her room, where the message of the willow tree echoed in her mind as she studied the collage of data taped to her door. The business with Mr. Archer made her understand how naive she had been. She needed to be more discerning.

She retrieved the business card Sergeant O'Donnell had given her and left for the police station, wearing her photographer's vest and carrying her backpack.

Sergeant O'Donnell listened to her story about Mr. Archer patiently.

"I knew something was missing from the backpack after it was stolen," Emma told him. "This morning I remembered what it was—the directions to the ARN office." Emma explained her search for her birth parents.

"You think that Archer hired these people," the policeman said, consulting his notes, "the Brennans, to set you up?"

"I don't know." Emma produced the license plate numbers. "It just seems like too many coincidences. I'd like to find out if these people really are who they say they are."

"Why wouldn't they be?"

Emma shrugged. "I was raised by a very wealthy family back home. I'll be coming into my inheritance now. They must be after my money." Emma was not ready to tell Sergeant O'Donnell about the owl torque, at least not yet.

"I see." Sergeant O'Donnell waved Emma into a seat by his desk. "Stay here. I'll see what I can do."

Emma watched as he pounded away on his computer keyboard with two stubby fingers.

"The blue Mercedes is registered to a Dublin man named John Cohan," said the police officer. "And the black Rolls-Royce belongs to a Mr. Victor Moore." Sergeant O'Donnell punched more keys. "Moore is an international jewel thief who specializes in selling antiquities on the black market to the highest bidder. He's been linked to a number of high-profile thefts—from your hometown, Chicago, to Leningrad. But he's slick: the police have never been able to catch up with him."

"So I was right."

"It appears so." Sergeant O'Donnell gave Emma a fierce look. "This Moore character is dangerous. A young woman like you—"

"I'll be just fine, Sergeant."

"What are you planning to do?"

Emma sighed. "Go home, I suppose, unless I can find out something more about my birth parents."

"An excellent idea," the policeman said firmly. "You do just that."

Back at Danu House, Emma thought about following Sam and Sergeant O'Donnell's advice and catching the next plane home to Chicago. But before she did, she wanted to wrap up a few loose ends. First, she tried to return the calls made to her the evening before. Devin did not answer. Emma was sorry about that; she would have liked to tell him good-bye in person before she left Dublin. The message from the Brennans she ignored. She did get through to Father Michael, the parish priest in County Meath.

"I remembered something that might prove of interest to you," he told her over the phone. "Why don't you drive out here for lunch and we'll discuss it?"

Emma agreed, despite her earlier resolve to go home right away. This was her last chance to solve the riddle of her past, and she was going to take it. Eager to hit the road, she left early, Mrs. Kelly's warning to trust no one ringing in her ears.

His father always told him that women were impossible creatures—unknowable. "Don't even try to understand them, son," he would say to Sam. "Just accept them as they are or you'll drive yourself crazy."

Sam rarely agreed with his father about anything, and he was loath to agree with him this time.

Sam had spent a lonely night in a small inn close to Shannon International Airport. He hadn't slept much. He'd tossed and turned in the Irish feather bed, dreaming of his beautiful Emma and denouncing her at the same time.

Now he stood at the gate where his Aer Lingus jet was waiting to carry him back home to Chicago. He approached the pretty redheaded flight attendant, his boarding pass in hand. He looked at her friendly freckled face. She smiled at him, cordial but contained. Her self-possession reminded Sam of Emma.

She was an independent girl, his Emma. But Sam believed that the independence she wore like a medal hid a loneliness, a loneliness intensified by the tragic events of the past few months. If only she would let her guard down long enough for him to ease that loneliness, he knew he could help her lose it forever.

But Emma was nothing if not relentless.

Just accept them as they are. Sam heard his father's ironic words echo in his head.

"Your boarding pass, please." The flight attendant smiled again; this time her green eyes caught Sam's and held them. They were the same emerald green as Emma's, the same emerald green as the owl torque's single blinking eye. He held out his boarding pass for the smiling attendant to inspect.

I can't do it, he thought. *Archer won't quit until he gets the owl piece—and he won't care whether Emma gets in the way or not. I can't leave her.*

He left the pretty redhead standing with his boarding pass still in her hand.

"Sir," she called after him as he bounded away from the gate. "Sir!"

Sam kept on running. He only hoped he wasn't too late.

"You sent me to County Cork for nothing?" Devin asked his mother, his Irish temper flaring. At his mother's insistence, he'd driven across the country to County Cork to see his favorite cousin, whom his mother said was very ill. When he'd found his cousin Grady in bed with a mild case of the flu, he'd turned right around and raced home to Dublin to confront his mother.

His mother regarded him with the regal stare only a mother could accomplish. "Do not speak to me in that tone, Devin O'Connor."

"But Mama, Grady was fine." Devin lowered his voice to an intense stage whisper. He looked at his mother, who stood before him as polished and poised as always. "You made me leave Emma after she was attacked."

"I didn't know anything about that," Maeve protested.

"No," conceded Devin. "But even if you had, you would have sent for me. The truth is, you don't like her."

"That's not true," she said, her voice thick with emotion.

"Yes, it is. Is it because she's American?" Devin didn't wait for an answer. "It doesn't matter." He headed for the door. "I've got to go."

"Devin, stay, please." She followed him to the front door, placing her cool, slender hands on his broad shoulders.

He shook her off. "No. Emma needs me." He turned to face her. All his life they'd been inseparable, he and his mother. He loved and respected her, not least for the miracle she'd made of her life for his sake, so that he could have everything.

Well, he didn't want everything. He wanted Emma. She was special; he'd never felt that way about a girl before. He felt as if he'd known her all his life. She made sense to him in a way no other girl could. She understood him—and he understood her.

"Devin," his mother pleaded with him. "Don't go. You could be hurt."

Devin saw fear in his mother's eyes; he couldn't recall his mother ever revealing fear of any kind. What was she so afraid of? That he would leave her, go off to America with Emma? Maybe he would.

"I'm sorry, Mama," he said. "This is something I have to do. Alone."

With that, he was gone.

CHAPTER TWENTY-TWO

Michael sat alone at the holy well, waiting for Mary. It was the day they were going to elope to America. Knowing that his parents would try to stop them, they had told no one of their plans, continuing their separate lives as usual—Michael at the seminary and Mary at home. Michael's fellow seminarians would take their vows the next day, expecting him to be among them. He wouldn't be there, but his conscience was clear. He had made his peace with God; his place was with Mary and their baby. God would understand.

Michael looked at his watch. They were supposed to meet at the well at dawn. It was after six; the sun had been up for nearly an hour already. It was typical of Mary to be late, but Michael had hoped she would make it there on time. He was nervous about getting away, and he wouldn't rest easy until they were safely aboard the plane to America.

Michael regarded the stone walls of the holy well with affection. He would miss this sacred place. He would miss Ireland, every inch of which was sacred to him. But a life with Mary and the baby would more than make up for the loss of his homeland.

Reaching over to the statue of the Virgin Mary that stood on the edge of the wall, Michael removed the rosary a pilgrim had wrapped around it as a gift. He kissed the feet of Jesus on the rosary's crucifix and then crossed himself with it. While he waited, he would say the rosary—to thank God for the miracle of his beautiful Mary.

The pain had struck around midnight. At first Mary wasn't sure what was wrong; after all, the baby was not due for two months. She figured the cramps that clenched her womb must be false labor, probably brought on by her own excitement. Due to leave the house in a couple of hours to meet Michael, she had decided to wait the pain out. She lay very still in her narrow bed, biting her pillow when the pain was too much so that she wouldn't wake her sick mother or, worse, her drunk stepfather.

By two she realized that the pains were not going to stop coming. *Dear God,* she thought, *this is real labor. I'm going to have this baby, soon.* She had to get out of the house while she was still physically able to do so. She could wait for Michael at the well. He'd know what to do next.

"We've got to get out of here, sweet baby," she whispered. "Try to slow down a bit, won't you?"

She struggled out of her bed, grasping the iron bedstead for support. She stood there, breathing heavily, as another contraction came and went. The contractions were getting stronger and coming faster now; Mary knew she must hurry. She didn't bother changing clothes, but simply grabbed her coat and slipped it on over her nightgown.

Luckily, she'd packed earlier that evening, hiding her suitcase under the bed. Squatting down slowly, she reached under the iron frame to pull out the case. The scraping sound of the suitcase along the hardwood floors echoed loudly in her ears; Mary held her breath, praying that her stepfather would not awaken.

After a few moments of silence, Mary unsnapped the case and checked the baby blanket that lay across the top of the few clothes Mary owned. She'd made the blanket herself out of the finest cream-colored Irish wool, trimming it with matching pure silk satin binding. She felt along the binding at the right bottom corner of the blanket, where she'd sewn in her half of the Blathnait bracelet. It was still there. She snapped the suitcase shut again. Everything was ready.

"Time to go," she whispered to her baby. "You hold on now."

Mary made her way carefully out of her bedroom, one hand braced against the wall for support, the other holding the suitcase. She was halfway down the hall when another contraction struck her like a blow. Biting her lip to keep from crying out against the pain, Mary sank to her knees. *Mother of God,* she prayed, *help me.*

She had to get out of there, even if she did so on all fours. Mary waited for the contraction to finish its course. Then, still on her knees, she inched her way past her mother and stepfather's room and into the parlor. Another ten feet and she'd be out of the house. Using the strong arm of the sofa, she pulled herself up. Unsteady but on her feet, she headed for the door. Just as she reached for the doorknob, she felt a rush of warm liquid between her legs.

My water's broken, she realized with a panic. She clutched her swollen belly as another pain hit her, dropping the suitcase. Her head swam; multiple doorknobs filled her eyes. *Michael, forgive me,* she thought as she felt herself falling, falling, falling into darkness.

CHAPTER TWENTY-THREE

Devin pulled up in front of Danu House just as Sam stepped out of his cab.

"I thought you were leaving," Devin said to him as he approached the hotel.

Sam regarded his rival coolly. "I changed my mind."

Devin turned his back on Sam, bounded up the stairs, and rang the doorbell. Sam joined him. They stood there, broad shoulder to broad shoulder, waiting for Mrs. Kelly.

The door opened to reveal the indomitable Mrs. Kelly, who laughed out loud at the sight of them. "Good day, boys. And what might you two be doing here?" She winked. "Come to visit an old lady, have you? Come on in." She ushered them into the parlor. "Do sit down."

"We can't stay," said Devin. "Is Emma here?"

"I'm afraid not," said Mrs. Kelly.

"Where is she?" Sam asked.

Mrs. Kelly smiled at him. "I knew you would come back. The cards said so."

"Where *is* she?" Sam's voice was sharper now.

"She's gone. I don't know where she went." Mrs. Kelly frowned. "You boys should never have left her alone."

"You're right," Devin said. "Absolutely right."

"You don't have any idea where she went?"

"She was expected in Ballsbridge for luncheon," Mrs. Kelly said. "But then the priest called."

"Ballsbridge? Who could she know there?" Devin looked at Sam. Sam shrugged.

"The Brennans," answered Mrs. Kelly. "They say they are her birth parents."

Devin and Sam stared at her.

"She found them?" Sam had never really believed Emma would find out who she was. He was so glad he was wrong. "How?"

"Through the ARN office," said Mrs. Kelly.

"That's great," Devin said, grinning.

Mrs. Kelly frowned again. "Perhaps."

"What do you mean?" Sam cursed himself for leaving Emma alone.

"The cards point to deception," Mrs. Kelly said anxiously.

"What cards?" Devin turned to Sam. "What's she talking about?"

"Tarot cards," Sam explained.

"I see. Well now, Mrs. Kelly, would you have that address in Ballsbridge? We need to get on."

"Of course." She left the room, returning within minutes with a slip of notepaper. "Do be careful." She looked at Sam with shrewd eyes. "Once you find her, dear, keep her in sight."

"Yes, ma'am," said Sam.

The two young men said good-bye to Mrs. Kelly and stepped outside.

"You can ride with me in my van," Devin said to Sam as he attempted to flag down a cab.

In the interest of minimizing his expenditures, Sam agreed. "Thanks," he told Devin, all the while thinking that this way he could keep an eye on the brash Irishman.

Emma sped toward County Meath, enjoying the emerald beauty of the Irish countryside. The encounter with Sergeant O'Donnell had upset her. She had really liked the Brennans; worse, she had believed them. Emma didn't understand how anyone could lie that way. She remembered the way Mrs. Brennan's sweet face had lit up when she saw Emma. How could that woman pretend to be somebody's mother? *Her* mother. Emma choked back a sob. She was not going to waste any tears on that woman. She must have been a professional actress, Emma thought. She and Mr. Brennan both must have been. That must have cost some money, hiring real actors. So had chasing her halfway around the world.

It all came back to Mr. Martin, the jeweler back home. It was hard to believe that the Kenilworth jeweler would even know someone like Archer, much less do business with him.

She thought about Archer and the Brennans. They didn't know her; it was nothing personal with them. They were just greedy people willing to do anything for money.

But Mr. Martin had known Emma all of her life. He'd been her mother's friend. Those were the worst betrayals—the ones that struck so close to home. If Mr. Martin had betrayed her and her mother the way Grandmother Beatrice had betrayed them ... those were actions Emma could never forgive or forget.

She stepped on the gas, speeding down the isolated stretch of road with an uncharacteristic recklessness. The little Ford swerved, and Emma slowed down. *Maybe this is part of growing up,* she thought, *learning who your real friends are and who they aren't.*

Sam and Sally were her real friends—the only people left in the world who really knew her and loved her. And wherever she was, her mother, Grace, would always love her. *I must remember that,* Emma told herself. These people were her real family, and they were all she needed. Any other family she might find would be a wonderful addition to this family. But that's what they would be—an addition.

Emma felt better. True, she was disappointed that she had yet to find her birth parents. But better to suffer the disappointment than to wrongly embrace the Brennans as her parents. That would be the cruelest lie of all.

Maybe Father Michael could help. He might have been able to jog the aging Father Francis's memory. Perhaps the old man was ready to divulge whatever truth he could remember. Or maybe he'd found something in the church records. Emma knew that the parish kept records of all the baptisms of newborn babies. Catholics baptized their children as babies, and baptismal records were recognized as birth certificates by most governments.

There was no way of knowing whether her birth parents would have baptized her before giving her up for adoption, but among devout Irish Catholics it would not have been uncommon. Father Michael had only to review the parish's baptismal records. ...

Stop it, Emma told herself. *Stop speculating.* She'd be there soon enough; no use torturing herself with the possibilities. She tried to settle down and concentrate on the road. After nearly a week in Ireland, she handled driving on the wrong side of the road with some aplomb, but that didn't mean she could afford to let her mind wander.

It was then that she noticed the car. A sleek black Rolls-Royce had appeared several car lengths behind her.

Archer. Emma felt a shiver of fear. She straightened, leaning toward the steering wheel. Gripping the wheel with white knuckles, she floored the Ford and took the next curve full out. The tires squealed as the Ford tore to the right, swinging into the other lane.

Emma glanced into the rearview mirror as she steered the car out of the curve and slammed onto the straightaway. The Rolls had slipped from view temporarily, hidden beyond the bend.

But Emma knew it would be back. She had to make the most of the flat stretch of road before her. She pushed the gas pedal to the floor and held it there, roaring up the road as fast as the little Ford could carry her.

She checked the mirror again. There was the Rolls just rounding the curve. She smiled. If she could just make it to the church, she might be safe.

Up ahead the road narrowed sharply, snaking to the right. Emma did not lift her foot from the pedal, but braced herself for the curve. The car careened off the road and onto the shoulder. Emma held on to the steering wheel, willing the Ford to right its course. She pulled the wheel to the right, trying to maneuver the vehicle back on the road. The Ford came flying out of the curve, bouncing into the right lane. She sighed with relief at having made the turn, then screamed as she saw a truck barreling toward her. She yanked the steering wheel to the left. The driver of the truck swerved off the road; Emma missed him by mere inches.

She briefly considered going back to see if the driver was okay, but the rearview mirror showed the black Rolls thundering on in her wake. It was a good thing the truck driver had pulled onto the shoulder; the Rolls, too, had slid into the wrong lane rounding the hairpin curve.

Emma's heart sank as the engine began to sputter and cough. The little Ford was not built for such harsh travel. She slowed down a little, hoping a slight respite would soothe the rental car's engine.

The Rolls was gaining on her now, thanks to her slower speed. Frantic, Emma floored it again, desperate to cross the bridge that loomed ahead before the Rolls caught up with her. The little Ford had gained its second wind, and sped across the narrow old stone bridge well ahead of the Rolls.

But less than a mile down the road the Ford faltered again. Emma let up on the gas, and the relentless Rolls Royce narrowed the gap. To Emma's horror, the Rolls overtook her, passing on the right. The windows were darkly tinted; Emma could not see Archer inside, but she knew he was there.

And he was going to get her.

As this thought struck Emma like a physical blow, the Rolls slammed into the Ford.

The little car swayed off onto the shoulder of the road. Emma gripped the steering wheel, trying to pull the car back onto the road.

But she was too late. The Ford plunged past the shoulder of the road and down toward the stone wall that flanked the highway. Emma braced herself for the inevitable impact.

On the seemingly interminable drive to Ballsbridge, Sam resisted Devin's attempts to draw him into conversation. He was too worried about Emma to indulge in small talk. *The Irish talk too much,* he thought irritably as Devin asked him again about ARN and the Brennans.

"You know as much as I do," Sam told him. "Aren't we about there?"

"Just another block or so." Devin grinned at him. "Is it that you don't much care for the art of conversation, or you don't much care for me?"

Sam resisted the urge to blurt out, "Both." Instead he said simply, "I'm not a big talker."

"Ah," said Devin, "the all-American strong, silent type. I'm afraid we don't see much of your kind here in Ireland." He pointed to the fashionable Georgian house of the Brennans. "There it is. A lovely home, don't you think?"

"Yes." Sam regarded the house with relief. Maybe the Brennans were perfectly nice people after all. He'd been so afraid for Emma, afraid that if she did against all odds find her birth parents, she wouldn't like what she found.

Devin parked the car; together they strode up the stairs to the front door. Sam rang the bell.

The door opened immediately. The Brennans stood there, the picture of rich, comfortable suburbia. The Irish equivalent of Kenilworth people, Sam realized with a start.

"We're looking for Emma Lambourne," he told the woman.

"Who are you?" Mr. Brennan's voice was polite but distant.

"Oh, do excuse my friend, he's American." Devin stepped forward and offered Mr. Brennan his hand. "I'm Devin O'Connor and this is Sam Tyler. We're friends of Emma's. Sam here actually traveled from Chicago with Emma."

"Odd," said Mrs. Brennan, "she didn't mention anything about a young man. Did she, Patrick?"

"No, she didn't." Absently shaking Devin's hand, Mr. Brennan gave Sam a stern look.

"We know Emma's having luncheon here and we'd like to speak to her briefly if we could. We'll just be a moment." Devin smiled at them warmly.

"She's not here." Mrs. Brennan said. "She was due to arrive an hour ago. We were getting worried—"

"You look so familiar," Devin said suddenly to Mr. Brennan. "Do I know you?"

"I don't think so." Mr. Brennan frowned.

"She didn't call?" asked Sam.

"No, we haven't heard a word."

"That's not like Emma, to be so late and not call." Sam was getting worried, too.

"I know you from somewhere," Devin said, staring at Mr. Brennan openly.

"I don't think so," repeated Mr. Brennan. He turned to his wife. "There's really nothing we can do—"

"I've got it!" Devin snapped his fingers. *"The Playboy of the Western World.* Abbey Theatre. One—no, two seasons ago. You played the pub owner." He chuckled. "I never forget a face."

Sam stared hard at Devin. "Are you saying he's an *actor*?"

"That's right. And a pretty good one, as I recall. What's wrong with that?"

"Everything." Sam moved toward the older man. "If you did anything to hurt her—"

Mr. Brennan pushed his wife back roughly with one hand and slammed the front door in Sam and Devin's faces with the other.

Devin turned to Sam, perplexed. "What is going on?"

But Sam was already running down the stairs toward Devin's van. "Come on!" he yelled. "There's no time to waste. I'll explain everything on the way to the church."

CHAPTER TWENTY-FOUR

The Ford plunged over the shoulder of the road. Emma held her breath as the vehicle tore through the high wheat-colored grass and green hedges, only to crash to a stop as its nose hit the edge of the peat bog.

The blow threw Emma forward, knocking the wind out of her. Her seat belt dug painfully into her flesh but saved her from further injury. She gasped for breath, and gasped again. Shaken, she realized she was all right, but that she had to get out of there.

She looked around her. There was no sign of Archer. It was very quiet; the only sound was the hiss of the Ford's crumpled radiator. With unsteady hands Emma removed her seat belt. She struggled to open the door, but it wouldn't budge. She pushed and pushed; finally she panicked and punched it open with her feet.

She stumbled out of the car. She looked up and saw the Rolls-Royce approaching from the other direction. Archer must have swerved around the Ford to avoid collision, then turned back to come after her. He was too far away to have seen her get out of the car. Emma scrambled onto the peat bog and ran.

And ran. And ran. There was nowhere to hide. The peat seemed to stretch on into eternity. Still Emma ran.

Suddenly, out of the corner of her eye, she caught sight of a small wood. She shifted course abruptly, running for the blessed leafy cover.

Against her better judgment, she glanced back over her shoulder to see where her pursuer was. Archer was just exiting the Rolls-Royce. He did not look her way; his attention was focused on the Ford.

She didn't have much time. Emma turned her attention back to the task at hand, and sprinted for the wood. She ran hard, her sneakers sinking into the mushy peat, her jeans soaked above the ankles. Her ribs ached; every breath hurt.

Just when she thought she could go on no longer, Emma reached the edge of the wood. She stumbled through the brush, heading for the greater security of the trees. Clumps of bushes flanked the tree line. Emma sank into the middle of one such clump to catch her breath. Hidden from view, she watched Archer as he leaned over to inspect the Ford. He didn't find what he was looking for—Emma. He spun around and gazed out across the peat bog. Emma shivered under the weight of his stare, even though she knew he couldn't see her.

He stood there for a moment, seemingly undecided, then strode out across the bog toward the wood.

Toward Emma.

Emma didn't know what to do. The wood was a small one; if she stayed within it, Archer was sure to find her eventually. On the other hand, if she left it, she'd expose herself to Archer—a stupid move, especially if he carried a gun.

Either way she needed to get out of the bushes and into the trees. She crawled through the bushes, making her way slowly toward the tree line.

It was then that she saw them, a half dozen small scraps of cloth tied to the branches of a bush that looked no different from its neighbors. But it was different. The little lengths of fabric that waved their welcome to Emma were clooties. Hanging clooties on bushes and trees was an old Celtic custom; their presence indicated that there was a holy well nearby.

The clooties gave Emma an idea. Quickly she untied the pieces and slipped them into her back jeans pocket.

"I promise to put them back," she whispered to any faery people who might see her and object to their removal. Then she dropped to her stomach and crawled through the bristly undergrowth. Soon she found herself in a tiny clearing completely surrounded by high bushes. The clearing led down into the holy well.

It was a beautiful place, a place of peace and grace. The ancient well was built of centuries-old stone, which glistened under the tireless streams of cool water that trickled down into the pool at its bottom. A low stone wall bordered the pool; statues of Jesus and the Virgin Mary stood on this shelf, lending an official air to the natural sacred aura of the well.

Emma slipped down onto the damp stone wall and seated herself next to the statue of the Virgin Mary. She would stay there, she decided, and hide. Without the clooties to alert Archer to the presence of the well, maybe he would pass right by it. With any luck, he would search the woods for her and, finding nothing, return to his car. Then she could make her escape. Emma would simply wait him out.

Sam saw it first. "Oh, my God!"

"What?" Devin jerked his head at Sam. "What?"

Sam pointed toward the open road. "Up there on the left. It's the rental car."

"Oh, my God," echoed Devin. He stepped hard on the gas pedal and they sped ahead. "At least someone's pulled over to help her already."

"Maybe."

"What do you mean?"

"You're assuming that whoever stopped is a friend."

Devin's VW van roared past the Rolls-Royce and then screeched to a stop next to the Ford. The young men bounded out of the van and raced to the crumpled vehicle.

"She's not here." Devin frowned. "Maybe an ambulance took her away."

"I don't think so," Sam said. "There's no blood, nothing to indicate she's been hurt. Besides, from the look of this, Emma went this way." Sam showed Devin where someone had obviously pushed through the high grasses and bushes.

"You're right," Devin said, but Sam wasn't listening. Devin followed his gaze out across the peat bog to where a tall man was heading into the small wood.

Sam stepped forward, poised for flight.

Devin clapped a strong hand on his shoulder, holding him back. "Take the van and drive on down to the church. It's only another couple of miles at the most. Call the police."

"No way." Sam tried to shrug Devin's hand away, but Devin held firm.

"I have a better chance of finding her, Sam. I know this area well. I grew up around here." He released his grip and leapt forward. "Go for help," he said, and took off running.

Sam sighed. As much as he hated to admit it, Devin was right.

"Hold on, Emma," he whispered, and headed for Devin's van.

Emma sat on the damp stone wall, her long, jean-clad legs dangling over the edge, her bare toes skimming the top of the pool. Her fear of discovery had subsided with each passing uneventful moment; now, after what she gauged to be half an hour or so, she felt quite at home.

There was something familiar about the place. She couldn't put her finger on it, but it would come to her, sooner or later. Emma leaned her head back against the cold stone and closed her eyes. She felt safe there, protected. She had never been a particularly religious person, but she could understand why religious people would seek out such a place, as they had done for centuries.

Emma had read a lot about the holy wells of Ireland. Many had been considered sacred since time immemorial.

Ancient peoples had worshiped such sources of water, because without them they would have died. Holy wells like these were natural shrines to the mother goddess. The ancient Celts would have worshiped Celtic goddesses such as Danu and Brigit and Deirdre there. Modern Irish Catholics paid homage to the Virgin Mary and St. Brigid and St. Deirdre. Over the years the names had changed along with the religion of the people—but the spirit remained the same.

Emma opened her eyes and gazed out at the strange little oasis in which she found herself. She thought that Mrs. Kelly would like it there. She wondered if all of the holy wells were as beautiful as this one. She wished she had her camera with her—she could shoot some great shots there. But in her hurry to get out of the car she'd left it behind. Still, she could dream her photography—something she often did when the world surprised her with great beauty and she was without her trusty Nikon.

For that she needed only her imagination, and she could frame countless perfect shots of the well right in her head: that upper right corner where long curls of ivy traversed the gray rock; the serene statue of the Virgin Mary, bedecked with a pilgrim's rosary; the far stone wall, its top half lit by a rare bit of Irish sun, its bottom half darkened by shadow and the unceasing trickle of spring water.

It was that picture—of the far wall, steeped in partial shadow—that Emma had seen before. That was why the place seemed familiar to her.

And suddenly Emma remembered where she had seen it. At the rectory, in Father Michael's parlor, hanging on the wall with the photographs of nearby Newgrange.

The thought of Father Michael's photograph cheered her—why, she couldn't really say. Perhaps it was a well many of the local pious townspeople frequented; perhaps Father Michael himself would wander by and rescue her.

Either way, she promised herself that if she was lucky enough to get out of this alive, she'd take the next plane back to Chicago, home to Sam and Sally.

Until then, she looked to the mother goddess to protect her.

CHAPTER TWENTY-FIVE

Sam screeched to a stop in front of the church. He threw open the door and bounded out of the van, sprinting past a gray Audi to the rectory entrance. He slowed down long enough to pound a warning on the heavy wooden door, then burst inside.

He found himself in a hallway; he looked desperately around him, trying to decide which way to go next.

"May I help you?" A priest appeared from the room to the left; an attractive woman about Sam's mother's age stood behind him.

"Where's your phone?" Sam's voice was brusque.

"It's in my office," answered the priest patiently. "May I ask—"

"I need to call the police," Sam cut in. "Look, we don't have much time. Emma's in trouble. As soon as I call the police, I'll explain."

The priest nodded, and without a word led Sam to a small office at the back of the rectory. Sam contacted the local police, as well as Sergeant O'Donnell in Dublin. Satisfied that he had done all he could do there, he prepared to leave.

The woman blocked his way. "What is this all about?"

She must be somebody's mom, Sam thought. *She sounds just like a worried mom.* "Sorry. I'm Sam Tyler from Chicago." He stuck out his hand awkwardly.

The woman shook his hand warmly. "I'm Maeve Collins and this is Father Michael."

Sam nodded, trying to cut the pleasantries short. "I came here to Ireland with Emma Lambourne, to help her find her birth parents. A guy followed us here from America—a bad guy—and I think he's kidnapped Emma. We found her car abandoned along with his on the side of the road about a mile south of here."

"We?" asked the woman.

"Devin O'Connor, this goofy friend of Emma's."

The woman smiled. "I wouldn't call him goofy, exactly."

"You know him?"

"He's my son."

"Oh." Sam didn't know what to say to that.

"Is he in the van?"

"No. He's back in the woods now, looking for them. He says he grew up around here, that he can find them. But he's going to need help. That's why I need to get back there right away."

"Oh, God." Her voice was faint. Sam headed for the door.

"Why is this man after Emma?" asked the priest.

Sam turned. "He wants the bracelet." He held up his hands in frustration. "Look, it's a long story. Too long to go into right now."

The woman and the priest exchanged glances.

"The holy well," they whispered in unison.

A twig snapped, and Emma stiffened. She heard the slow, heavy step of a man searching for something. *Archer,* she thought, sitting absolutely still. Then a second set of footsteps sounded—quicker, harder, younger. *Who could this be?* Emma thought wildly.

All the footsteps stopped abruptly. Emma heard an odd smack, then a loud thud. What was going on out there? Emma briefly considered venturing into the woods, but decided to stay put. No reason to reveal herself unnecessarily.

A shot rang out. Emma scrambled to her feet, nearly slipping on the damp stone wall. Cursing, she willed herself to remain immobile. She waited, breathless, and listened so hard it hurt.

No more shots, just an obscure scuffling noise. Emma shivered in spite of herself.

"Emma Lambourne, present yourself," a voice called out in a rich Continental accent Emma would have known anywhere.

It was Archer.

She said nothing; she'd wait him out, as planned. He'd never find her there.

"Miss Lambourne, I have your friend here with me. Unfortunately I find it necessary to press a revolver to his head. I won't hesitate to use it. Now, present yourself."

Stunned, Emma deliberated. Could he really have Sam with him? How? Sam was on his way home to Chicago.

"Miss Lambourne, I am not a man of great patience. Do not test me."

Emma heard muffled voices, then a sharp cry.

"I fear your friend has suffered a rather nasty blow to the brow, Miss Lambourne. I do suggest you stop this unnecessary violence at once."

"Don't do it, Emma!" The Irish lilt was unmistakable. It was Devin.

Emma's heart sank as she heard Devin let out another sharp cry of pain. She couldn't let Archer hurt him any more.

She crept in silence to the entrance to the holy well. "Okay, Mr. Archer, okay," she called out. "Just leave him alone, please."

"Come out where I can see you," commanded Archer.

Emma stepped through the bushes. Archer stood to her right; Devin lay on the ground at his feet, unconscious.

"Devin," she whispered, and ran to him.

Archer stopped her just short of Devin with a wave of his gun. "Stay away from him."

"But he's hurt. What did you do to him?" Gun or no gun, Emma was angry and she didn't hide the fact.

"He's just taking a little nap. He'll be awake in no time." Archer laughed at his little joke. "Miss Lambourne, you know what I want. Simply give it to me and I'll be on my way."

"I, I—"

"Give it to me." Archers voice had lost its cultivated tone. He sounded grittier and meaner now.

"I don't have it with me."

"You're lying." He stepped forward, the revolver pointing straight at her.

"I'm not lying. Let's go back to the car and I'll—"

"Take off the vest."

"What?"

He eyed her shrewdly. "Take off that vest."

She shrugged off her photographer's vest. "It's not there," she told him as she held the vest out to him.

He snatched it from her hand and backed away from her. Holding the gun under his arm, he searched the vest, tearing through the many pockets one by one, letting Emma's things fall where they might. Film, lens cleaner, filters, tissues, batteries—they fell like confetti, littering the ground at Archer's feet.

Emma stared past him to the edge of the tree line, where she could see three figures approaching. Archer couldn't see them; his back was to them.

Two of the people disappeared into the shadows; one lone figure continued on toward her. Archer was still busy destroying her vest, but that wouldn't occupy his interest for long. He'd run out of pockets soon.

She sneaked another look at the approaching stranger. She could see now that it was a young man; she realized with a start that it was Sam. Her heart leapt at the sight of him. She didn't know how or why he was there, but was she glad to see him! He would help her—he always did. But how could she warn him about the gun?

"It's not here." Archer threw the vest down, took the gun out from under his arm, and pointed it at Emma's heart. "Where is it?"

"I told you it wasn't there." Emma had to keep him talking; Sam was almost upon them.

"You said something about the car." He waved the gun at her. "Come on, let's go."

Terrified that he would turn and see Sam, Emma tried to distract him. "Not yet."

"What do you mean, not yet?" He stepped toward her, his dark eyes small and mean. "If I say go, you go."

"Sorry. I assumed you wanted both pieces of the torque."

That stopped him in his tracks. He smiled. "You've found the other half?"

Emma nodded.

"What a clever girl you are. Where is it?"

Her mind racing, Emma pointed to the bushes. "In there."

Archer's eyes narrowed. "What do you take me for, a fool?"

"Through those bushes is a holy well. That's where the other half is hidden. I was just about to get it when you called me out."

"Nonsense. You were hiding from me."

"Of course. The holy well is the perfect hiding place. How do you think I knew where to hide?"

Archer considered this for a moment. Emma held her breath as Sam stood in the shadows only a few feet from him, waiting for an opportune time to disarm him.

"Where's the other half?"

"In a safe-deposit box in a bank in Dublin."

This answer seemed to satisfy him. "I see." Archer tapped her shoulder with the gun. "Go on then, lead the way."

Emma turned, parting the bushes with her hands. She could feel Archer's breath on her neck. Where was Sam? She stepped into the thick brambles with Archer right behind her.

Whoosh! A rush of air signaled Sam's sideways attack on Archer.

"What the hell—?" said Archer, falling to Emma's right.

To her dismay she saw that despite Sam's tackle Archer still held the gun in his hand. She stomped on his wrist with all her might.

She heard the bones crack; Archer cried out in pain, and the gun slipped from his fingers. Emma pounced on it.

Sam punched Archer right on the nose as he struggled to get up. He fell back onto the ground. Sam flopped down on his chest to keep him there. Archer flailed his limbs, but Sam sat heavily upon him; he couldn't move.

"Hold the gun on him, Emma."

"Sam—" Emma looked at his nice all-American face and laughed with relief. "Boy, am I glad to see you."

He grinned at her. "Same here." Still seated on Archer, he twisted around to wave at the two figures who had reappeared at the tree line. At his gesture they broke into a run. Sirens sounded in the background.

The next several minutes were complicated and confusing. The two figures turned out to be Father Michael and Devin's mother. They went straight to Devin, who, roused by the ruckus, was groggy but conscious. The police came and took Archer away.

"We have to get Devin to a hospital," Maeve said.

"Mama," Devin said. "What are you doing here?"

Maeve said nothing.

"Mama?" Devin persisted.

"I came to see Michael—that is, Father Michael," Maeve said.

"How do you know Father Michael?" Emma was even more curious now.

"It's a long story," said Maeve, smiling.

Father Michael reached over and squeezed Maeve's hand. It was an oddly intimate gesture. Emma flushed with the realization that they were more than just friends.

Chapter Twenty-Six

Father Michael smiled at Emma. "We'd better tell them everything before they figure it out for themselves."

Emma glanced at the dazed Devin, who shrugged at her.

"Figure what out?" he asked.

"A long time ago, Mary Maeve and I were in love," began Father Michael. "We were kids, playing in the ancient ruins together and dreaming about our future. We were very young and very foolish, and very much in love."

Maeve turned to Devin. "But Michael was already promised to the Church, though he had not yet taken his vows. And I was planning on going to America to make a new life."

"You didn't want to be together?" Emma asked.

"I wanted nothing more than to be with Michael, but—" Maeve stopped.

"But a vow to the Church is not something a Catholic Irishman breaks lightly," Father Michael answered sadly. "I took my vows thinking I'd never see Mary Maeve again. And I didn't. Not until today."

"I knew Michael was lost to me, so I decided to marry a boy named Sean Leahy and go to America," said Maeve. "Then I realized I was pregnant. Sean knew the baby wasn't his, and left me. I sent a message to Michael, and he promised to meet me at the holy well and go off to America with me. We planned to use the torque to pay our way."

"Where did you find it?" asked Sam.

"In the ruins, not far from the holy well. It was buried under a pile of rocks."

"But you never went to America together," Emma said slowly. "What happened?"

"Mary Maeve never showed up to meet me," answered Father Michael. "I thought she'd abandoned me, so I returned to the seminary and was ordained into the priesthood the next day."

"I missed our meeting because I went into premature labor," explained Maeve. "It was a difficult labor; I was very ill for days afterward. By the time I was fully conscious, my stepfather had sold my babies. He said he didn't want any more mouths to feed."

"Babies?" Devin looked confused.

Emma remembered the birth records from County Meath. "Twins."

Maeve smiled. "That's right. I managed to locate my son and get him back, but my daughter had completely disappeared." She looked at Emma helplessly. "I was heartbroken. I knew Michael would say it was God's will. I tried to believe that, to be grateful that I had at least found my son and not hope for too much happiness."

"Why didn't you say something when I came to see you at the museum?" Emma asked, not knowing whether to be hurt or angry or both.

"I panicked," Maeve said. "Seeing you there—the picture of my mother—I was afraid of the truth I'd been trying to forget all these years." Her voice dropped to a whisper. "I'm so sorry."

Devin's mother. Emma struggled to take it all in. *Devin's mother is my birth mother.* She looked at Maeve Collins with new eyes, and saw her own glorious auburn hair and almond-shaped green eyes.

Devin stared at them. "Are you saying what I think you're saying?"

Maeve nodded. "Emma is your twin sister."

Devin stared at Emma, who returned his earnest gaze. Then he grinned. "Miss America is my sister."

"Why do you and Devin have different last names?" Emma asked, grinning back at Devin.

Maeve sighed. "I wanted Devin to bear the name of his ancestors, the O'Connors," she explained. "But I took the name Collins when I moved to Dublin to make a new life for myself and my child. I wanted to put my past behind me."

Devin's grin faded. "You always said my father was dead," he told his mother, his voice sharp.

"I know. I was wrong to lie to you." Maeve flushed. "He *was* dead, at least to me. He belonged to God. For years I hated him and his God."

"I never knew what happened," said Father Michael quietly. "I thought only that God had spoken, saying that Mary Maeve was not to be mine. And that I should serve the children of God, since I would never know my own children."

"How sad," Emma said.

Father Michael smiled. "I have prayed for this day all these years, never dreaming it would come."

"This is all going to take some getting used to," Devin said.

"What about the bracelet?" Sam asked.

"I had sewn my half into the baby blanket I made before I gave birth," said Maeve. "I needed a safe place to keep it away from my stepfather." She smiled at Emma. "It went with you and your adoptive parents. Your mother must have found it and kept it for you."

Emma nodded, remembering how Grace Lambourne had saved the gold owl piece for her all these years. "She was a wonderful person," she said. *And a wonderful mother,* she thought.

"What about the other half of the torque?" asked Sam.

"I suppose it's still where I hid it for Michael all those years ago," said Maeve. "I know as a curator I should have retrieved it and presented it to the museum. I thought about it many times, but I never really thought it was my place to do so. It was Michael's half of the torque, not mine." Her voice softened. "And I suppose part of me hoped that someday he'd come for it—and for me." She looked at Emma. "As for where I hid it—"

"Don't tell me," Emma said, thinking of her bluff to Archer. "Let me guess—at the holy well. That's where you used to meet, isn't it?"

Maeve and Father Michael smiled their assent.

"Let's go," Devin said, struggling to his feet.

"Devin, you need to rest." His mother's voice was firm.

"Come on." Devin turned to Emma for support. "Sis?"

Emma grinned. "If you're anything like me, and you must be, there's no stopping you."

She showed him the way through the bushes. The rest followed.

"It's beautiful," Sam said when they entered the holy well.

"It hasn't changed a bit," Maeve said. She slid down onto the damp stone wall, then moved to the corner, where she pulled an old brick from the wall. "You do the honors," she said to Emma.

Emma reached in and felt around in the dirt. "It's here," she said excitedly, pulling out the long-lost other half of the torque. "After all these years, it's still here."

"I can't believe it," Father Michael said.

Emma brushed off the dirt, then rubbed the gold piece with the soft cotton of her T-shirt until it gleamed. She held it up for them to see. "It's as beautiful as its twin."

Two hours later Emma and Sam joined Father Michael and Maeve at Devin's bedside in the hospital, where he was being kept overnight for observation.

"Come on, Emma, where is it?" Devin pressed.

"You must have hidden it well," Sam said.

"Not really," Emma said. "I just put it somewhere I knew Archer would never look." With a flourish she opened up the film compartment of her camera and retrieved her half of the torque. She pieced it together with shaking hands. "It's incredible," she whispered, staring at the delicate gold face of the Flower Daughter. "Just incredible."

"Put it on," Sam said. "Just once."

Emma slipped it on her pale wrist. "A perfect fit."

"Lovely," Father Michael said, "just like you."

Flushing, she took the torque off and gave it to Maeve. "You keep it, for the museum."

"Are you sure?" Maeve regarded her with the same tenderness with which she tended the ailing Devin. "After all you've been through, you might want to keep it."

Emma smiled at this enigmatic woman who had given birth to her, only to lose her. Until that day. "I don't need it," Emma said. "I found what I was looking for." She gave her birth mother a hug. "The torque belongs to Ireland."

"Thank you," Maeve said, hugging Emma tightly. "You know, as hard as I tried not to, all these years I've wondered where you were and how you were doing. As I watched Devin grow up, day by day, year by year, I pictured you growing up, too. Even in those daydreams, I never imagined a more wonderful young woman."

"There *is* no one more wonderful than Emma," Sam said.

Emma smiled at him and took his hand. "I have one more question," she said, addressing Maeve and Father Michael. "Was my real name really Emerald?"

Father Michael and Maeve nodded.

"We had an agreement," explained Father Michael. "If the baby was a boy, Maeve could name him; if it was a girl, I could."

"I chose *Devin,* which means 'poet' in Gaelic," Maeve said, "in the hope that he, like his father, would have the soul of a poet."

"And I chose *Emerald,*" said Father Michael, "because I hoped my daughter would have her mother's emerald eyes."

"Which she does," said Sam.

"Which she does," echoed Father Michael, smiling.

Emma smiled, happy that her search for her identity had led her to these fine people.

May 11,1994

Dear Sally,

You can stop worrying now. Everything has worked out better than I could ever have imagined.

Madame Rose was right about everything! I have found my mother and father—wonderful people—and a twin brother I never knew I had! Remember Devin, the cute Irishman I told you about? Well, he's my brother!

We also found the other half of the torque. I wish you could see how beautiful the whole bracelet is when you put the two halves together!

Archer, the international jewel thief who's been after the owl piece, is behind bars. You'll be happy to know that even though Archer was the man at Martin's Jewelry, the police have cleared Mr. Martin of any wrongdoing. (Another fine Kenilworth citizen retains his good name!)

We'll be staying on another couple of days. I want to spend some time with my newly discovered family. Plus I'm officially presenting the torque to the Republic of Ireland the day after tomorrow. They're even granting me honorary citizenship.

After that, we'll head back to Chicago. I can't wait to see you and tell you everything. *It's funny, but in coming to Ireland to find out who I was, I also found out where I belong—home in Chicago with my original family, you and Sam.*

See you soon.

Love,
Emerald

About the Author

Paula Munier Lee lives in Northern California with her husband and their four children. Of Irish descent, she is an active believer in tarot cards, leprechauns, and the proverbial pot of gold.

Made in the USA
Las Vegas, NV
19 March 2021